Last Words
Beyond The Wallace's

Carey Anderson

ISBN:0692577653
ISBN-13:9780692577653

DEDICATION

To *MY* MALCOLM! You have been the back bone to the Wallace Family since the beginning. Each story isn't about you, and yet each story is about you. You are key to the Wallace's prosperity and they see and acknowledge that.

This glimpse into your childhood was a lot harder than I thought it would be to write. I know you told me that you didn't know love as a small child, however reading between Pam's lines still proved to be very difficult to get through.

I am so thankful that you found the Wallace's and did not become another statistic in all aspects of your life. I am personally proud of the growth that you made despite your beginnings. Proof that if you're determined, and given the proper tools anyone can rise above what they've known.

I hope that you continue to allow love in your life. I hope that you continue to thrive on that love. I wish you all the success in the world. Like you, I try to rise above the map that was chosen for me. Like you, I plan to live free of the chains they tried to shackle me with. Like you, I will succeed. Like you, I will dare to dream and have more for me, not because I want it, but because I deserve it. Thank you *My* Malcolm for showing me the way. I love you *My* Malcolm!

Cover design: N.Alycia

Join me on Facebook –
www.facebook.com/careythewriteranderson

Twitter - @CareyTheWriter

Blog - http://careyanderson.blogspot.com

Website – http://www.careythewriteranderson.com

Photography by – Carey Anderson

ACKNOWLEDGMENTS

I would like to thank my baby-girl who is my life's ultimate expression of a dream realized. Thank you for sacrificing mommy time so that I could have the time to work some things out on paper.

I would like to thank my Soul Sistah #1 who has been my captivated audience since middle school. Without your love, support, encouragement, and FIRE I never would've completed Volume I or II, etc. Thank you for bringing me laughter when I couldn't get outside of my head.

I would like to thank my Sister-In-Law for taking time out of your busy family life to humor me with a read through of my latest thoughts and expressions. (SS1 & SIL THANK YOU for the trip to St. Helena where we spent the day lost in my imagination. I will never forget it, and it was exactly what I needed. THANK YOU!)

I would like to thank my dear cousin for reassuring me that my little hobby was relatable and entertaining. You are definitely a speed-reader, thank you for taking time out of your busy life to be entertained by my imagination.

I would like to thank last but not least Mrs. Laverne Dyes! Mrs. Dyes the day that you read my short story to my class changed my life. Thank you for giving me a positive outlet for all the angst going on in my life. You have forever changed my life, I am so thankful to have ever known you

Chapter 1

I don't even remember falling asleep. I remember that Mexican
putting something over my nose and as I tried to fight it went dark.
I was dreaming about everything and everybody. I awoke to
whomever this guy is taking me out of this car. He firmly put me
in this room with no windows. I wonder if this is all a garage. Are
we in a house, or some random place? I'd ask but he doesn't look
like he'd answer. He's a big unfriendly looking man. I doubt I
could take him, and his eyes are telling me not to even try. My
eyes burn and I feel, I feel, I'm scared. I don't understand what's
going on. All I do know is that I am about to die, and I don't
understand why.

If I had it to do over, I'd change everything. The only thing that is
hard to regret is... Have you ever loved someone that was no good?
Someone that no matter how bad they were to you, you just
couldn't leave them alone? That's how I felt about him. You see he
was my sister's man at the time. He made her so happy and he was
so fine. His skin was so smooth and deep cocoa colored. I've never
seen such a beautiful brown on someone's skin before or since. His
voice, I shiver when I think of it. Then there was Archie, the
biggest poindexter square I will ever meet in my life, or at least
that's how he started. When he finds out about this, I know he's
going to be heartbroken. I promised him it was going to be
different. He didn't want me to go have breakfast with my
momma. He didn't want me to deal with my family. I guess I
should've listened. I hate that it all has to end this way, but I'm
honestly relieved that it's over. I'm tired of this life anyways.

"Take this!" The very unfriendly man said handing me a fist full of
pills. Then he gave me a glass of something brown.

"Please tell Malcolm I'm sorry!" I pleaded.

"No talking! Drink!" He said then he sat down watching me.

"I didn't know who she was. My momma said that girl stole her money." The guy's expression didn't change. He stared at me like he didn't care. I took all the pills. "Now what?"

"You're going to sleep. Then I'm going to bury you."

"Where am I?"

"Does it matter?"

"You're not going to shoot me?"

"As long as you don't try anything, you'll get sleepy then you'll sleep. This is the most humane way, don't you think?"

"Malcolm hasn't called?" I held on to hope.

"He called." He watched my face.

A large range of emotions settled on me. My son is going to let me die. My son! He doesn't even care about my life. Fuzzy let them take me away, anger mixed with my fear. "He too scared to do it his self?"

"He'll be here shortly."

"Since this is it, can I tell you my side of the story? This is probably the last conversation I'll have with anyone."

He stared at me with an irritated look. I took his silence to be an agreement. I cleared my throat.

"My momma said the girl stole from her. I guess she meant the girl stole Malcolm." I exhaled, "do you love your momma?" He stared but didn't reply. "I hate mine! She's evil! I hope you beat her and when she's on the verge of healing you beat her again. I hope she dies the most painful death! Don't give her a humane death. Push her out the window and let the dogs feed on her!" Tears filled my eyes, "she's the modern day Jezebel. She was beautiful and still is evil!" I let my tears fall, tears I had been holding in FAR TOO LONG! I looked at the unfriendly guy hoping that my tears had some affect on him. I looked into his eyes and they were dark brown and cold. He didn't care, "tell Belinda everything she thought about me is true. It would be pointless to apologize, because my heart isn't truly sorry for it. I apologize for hurting her though." He looked at his watch, no doubt wanting me to shut up. "Seems like everybody's telling their stories these days. Here's mine..."

~

My sister and I got along ok I guess until this one day. Let me see... Oh yea... There was this one time when a girl said she wanted to fight my sister cause she stole her little bunny that she carries in her school bag. I told her my sister didn't steal her bunny. I told her my sister don't need her funky bunny. Everybody believed her and thought my sister did it. I know she didn't do it though. I know because I stole it. I didn't even really want the bunny or cared too much about it. She acted like this little stuffed animal was real. She acted like it talked to her and it has feelings or something. The bunny seemed like it made her happy and I wanted to feel like that. I wanted to see if the bunny would make me happy too. When it didn't, I ripped it up into little pieces and threw it away in the school trash. Why my sister got to be a thief though? Why my sister got to be the one? Like I couldn't possibly be the one? She was over there crying and snotting over the stupid bunny. She said she wanted to fight my sister and I'm like "I told you she didn't do it." But she wanna be stupid and fight her anyways, it's her funeral. My sister Belinda doesn't mess with anyone, but if they come to her she will send their body back return to sender. This girl was stupid. I don't even know why she picked Belinda, but who am I to understand the mind of a stupid person.

"You stupid tar baby! You stole my bunny!" The stupid girl yelled at my sister.

"Your what?"

"You heard me!" Then she charged.

Belinda grabbed her by her hair and she beat that stupid girl in the face until a teacher came and made her stop. She beat that girl so badly it was a shame. We sat over to the side watching and laughing. Once Belinda got going it was hard to calm her down. Two more teachers had to come to remove her. The rest of us stood to the side watching. If Belinda would've let this stupid girl beat her she never would've heard the end of it.

Everybody left but I waited for Belinda, I guess I kind of felt bad for her fighting like that. Belinda was still mad when we walked home she kept rolling her eyes at me. When we got home everybody was on the porch. Momma had people in the house; we aren't allowed to go in when her friends are there.

One time when we were in the house one of her friends got mad about something. He was cursing and yelling and when I came in the kitchen he burned me with his cigar on my arm. Momma said that was what I got for coming in the kitchen. But then he got mad again at my momma and she ended up stabbing him and telling him to find his way to the hospital if he could make it in time.

My burn hurt really bad, I couldn't sleep cause the sting of it kept waking me up. She whooped me for crying all night and told me to shut up. When my daddy finally came home he asked what was wrong with me. I showed him my burn and he cleaned it, put some aloe on it from momma's aloe vera plant and he told me to do this in the morning and at night. This was probably the only loving gesture he ever did in regards to me. Then he asked me what I did to get burned. I just said I was in the wrong place at the wrong time. If I told him what happened he wouldn't care, and I'd get in trouble for telling on her. So needless to say we knew to stay outside.

We were waiting outside and Belinda kept staring at me. So I started staring back. "Why you didn't tell her it was you?"

"Me what?"

"You stole her bunny."

"No I didn't!" How did she know?

"Yes you did! I saw you with the same stupid doll she was describing to the principal! You always want other people's stuff!"

"No I don't!" I yelled back.

Then momma's workers started walking out the door. The women never looked at us, they kept their eyes low. The men on the other hand always looked at us and they'd tell my momma how pretty we all were. Slick would look at us long and hard. He always had a toothpick or something in his mouth. He'd almost drool at us. My momma wouldn't say anything she'd watch him as he circled us. Today was no different, here came Slick staring and drooling. Momma came busting out the house with murder in her eyes. It seem like she was airborne as she jumped off the porch and then she snatched one of the women by her wig. "Barb please!" The girl yelled.

"Where's the rest of it?"

"That's all of it I swear!"

When momma hit her you heard it. "You must think I'm stupid! You think I don't know how to count or something?"

"It was a slow day, and the last guy said he didn't have enough." She pleaded.

"You turning tricks for free?"

"No!"

Momma hit her again, "you're lying! Where's my money?" She hit her again.

"That's all I have."

"You's a lie!" Momma threw her on the ground. She ripped her bra off with her shirt; when she didn't find her money there she pulled her skirt down. There was money in the waist of her panties. Momma started beating on her some more. "Since you wanna be a thieving liar," she looked at my brother. "JJ! Take her in the backyard!"

"OK!" JJ smiled clapping his hands together.

"When he's done with you, you better get out there and bring me double this tomorrow cause you not eating or anything until I get my money." She looked at the rest of her girls, "does anybody else want to join her?" No one said anything. "I know how many tricks you all turn. Bring me my money!"

JJ took the girl in the backyard. Slick told the girls to get in the car. "Barb, when is Bam coming home?"

"Any minute now, you gonna wait?"

"I don't know, these little ones starting to look ripe they selves."

"Not yet Slick, stick to Bam."

"I'll be back, tell her to be ready." Then he got in the car.

Momma looked at us, "what's wrong with y'all?"

"Pam stole this girl's toy and the girl said I did it so I got to stay home tomorrow."

"Stop lying on me!" I yelled.

Momma looked at me like she could see through me. "So you got suspended?" Belinda shook her head yes. "You know I'm gonna beat you. I don't care what your excuse is. This is your chance. Get Pam, cause I'm getting you."

It seemed like as soon as the words came out of momma's mouth my sister was charging me. I ran to get my footing. When we fight we don't fight like sisters. If I don't get her, she's going to get me. Momma stood back watching us like we were putting on a show for her. Bam came running and made us stop. Momma got mad at her for stopping us. Momma was about to get her when she stopped. She frowned at Bam and said she was trying to make her get her so she wouldn't have the baby. Bam didn't say anything she looked at momma.

Bam was having a baby by Slick. She didn't want to have the baby, but Slick was happy. Bam has gotten in more fights and trouble trying to get rid of the baby than she ever has. Bam don't even like Slick. Momma sent him in her room one morning when she was sleep. Tricey and Jan already have babies too. Tricey brings her babies after they're born and gives them to momma, she has three already. Momma let's them lay low for a little while and then she makes them work in exchange for watching their kids. When daddy used to get mad about them having babies momma wouldn't say nothing. She'd let them get in trouble as if it was their fault, and then she'd get daddy to be nice again.

Daddy had a numbers ring that he ran. People liked playing

numbers with him cause they say he's fair. He has a spot by the water where people can come see dog fights, rooster fights, play craps, if there's a way to bet on it he's running it. Everybody knows Tip Latour.

They say my momma took my daddy from his first wife, I don't know if that's true or not. My daddy is a lot older than my momma, but whatever she wants she gets. She's not even all that nice to him, but he don't seem like he cares. My daddy isn't a handsome man, but my momma is very pretty. People said that's why we so pretty, she had it to spare.

One time a man call himself trying to sweet talk my momma. She smiled and let him go on and on about how he was the modern day Mandingo. He told her my daddy was too old to give it to her good anymore and that was why she stopped having babies. He told her she needed a friend. His mouth got dry he was talking so hard. She smiled, "are you done?" He smiled thinking she was going for his jive. "My man may be old, but there's nothing that a little young buck like you could ever do for me. First of all any man who has to talk himself up so much just to get between a woman's legs is no good. Looking at your pants you're too small to come behind my man. You see Tip was blessed from the Muthaland personally by the God's. He don't need to talk about it, the proof is right there in his pants. My man has the gift of a simple look. Every time he looks at me my love comes down. Look at all the kids we got, because I can't stay off him. I may be a lot of things, but my legs only spread for Tip. And you my friend need to stick to these young girls who don't know no better than to fall for your game."

"But he's old!"

She smiled, "and knows what he's doing."

The man looked embarrassed. "Don't matter cause he ain't doing it no more."

"Why do you keep saying that?"

"You ain't had no more babies."

"Not that it's any of your business, but I ain't have no more babies cause my body said no more. My man still gives it to me good every time he see me."

Some people say that my daddy heard about that guy approaching my momma and he got him. Other people say the guy tried to confront my daddy and he got him. Either way my daddy got him and we never saw that guy again.

****

It felt too crowded in the house, so I got up and got dressed. Little Fuzzy was sitting on the porch looking for his momma to come. She normally doesn't come and he gets sad. "What you doing?"

"Nuffin! You?"

"You wanna go wander around with me?"

"Yes!" He said with a smile. We walked for a while singing silly songs and being goofy. "Pam, I'm hungry." He grabbed his chubby stomach.

We went to the market; Fuzzy stood watch as I stole food for us. We had a picnic in the park devouring our food. As we ate I noticed Fuzzy staring at someone. It was a man with a little baby boy. "What?"

"I wish my daddy took me to the park." He watched with sad eyes.

"Maybe when Macio comes home, he can take you to the park."

Fuzzy smiled, "you think he will?"

We watched the guy play with his son for a little while, and then we left.

A couple weeks later Macio came home. Momma and Daddy were so happy when he came that they made sure they were both home when he got there. Macio had on his uniform and he saluted daddy, then he hugged momma. Momma hugged Macio so tight and kissed him. It made me mad, she never hugged and kissed me ever. I looked at my brothers and sisters and they all looked like they were thinking the same thing. Macio looked around, "look at all y'all. It's good to be home, even if I didn't think I'd be home so soon."

"Hush now! That was a mistake. It's their loss! I'm happy to have my baby home in one piece." Momma rubbed his shoulders.

Macio shook his head. Then he looked at JJ and Leroy. "I want to box both of you. Meet me out back, now!" Macio started pulling his tie loose and unbuttoning his jacket. "Where all these babies come from?" He asked as he laid his jacket down.

"Your sisters seem to like laying on their backs these days." My daddy said.

My sisters looked at momma and she stood there not saying a word as if it were true.

Daddy gave Macio and Leroy gloves. Daddy said everybody who thought Macio would win had to stand on the left and those betting on Leroy had to stand on the right. Leroy is pretty crazy, no one messes with him. Macio must've forgotten. Daddy said go, and Leroy came straight for Macio. Leroy came out firing on Macio and Macio let him. We thought Leroy was about to knock him out when Macio blocked his punch and then moved really fast firing on Leroy not giving him a chance to square up. Leroy went down and everybody was silent. Leroy was knocked out, and Macio told

JJ to hurry up. JJ got knocked down just like Leroy. Daddy asked Macio how he was doing this. Macio explained that they were all muscle and no brain. He said they were forgetting that he could be just as strong. Daddy told Macio he needed to teach his brothers. Macio's eyes got big. He said he liked the idea of having his own boot camp. Macio called little Fuzzy over, and then he told Fuzzy to punch his hand. When Fuzzy did his eyes got big with excitement. He got down on his knees. He showed Fuzzy how to punch and then he told him to do it again. Macio smiled at Fuzzy and told him he was a natural. He called all the other little boys over and he started barking orders and all the boys were eager to get a commendation from Macio. My parent's eyes got big as they looked on with approval.

Over the next month you saw muscles plumping up and chub falling off. Except for Fuzzy, it seemed like he just got stronger he remained chubby with muscles. Macio trained all my brothers in the backyard. Then he'd take all his nephews to the park per Fuzzy's request and he'd have them doing drills. As soon as they could walk Macio was taking them. My daddy started using my brothers as security at his spot, and sometimes momma would have my brothers pay people visits who owed her money. Pretty soon we started feeling like an army.

Chapter 2

I took another swallow of the brown. I looked at the guy who only mildly showed interest in my story. He was more or less waiting for these pills to do their job. I didn't feel anything yet so I decided to keep talking.

~

I was thirteen when Bam ran away. She had just had baby number four and she couldn't stop crying. Little Renee was sleeping with her when Bam sat up. She wiped her eyes, and then she looked around the room. She kept saying she had to get out, she couldn't stay here anymore. Tricey told her she'd feel better in the morning as the sleep in her voice pulled her back to sleep. Bam sat up like that for a long time like she was arguing in her head with herself. I laid there quietly watching my big sister on the verge of insanity. She looked at her babies then she stood up. She got dressed and then she walked out the room with her shoes in her hand. I thought she was going to the bathroom, but when I heard the front door I knew better. In the morning momma woke everybody up asking where Bam was. No one knew, momma didn't believe Tricey or any of us. We all got beat until she was satisfied that we didn't know. Then she told us we were getting beat until Bam came back. If we didn't hate Bam before, getting beat like this was definitely doing the trick. If I knew all of this was going to happen I would've told on her as soon as I heard the front door close.

A couple weeks later Slick came looking for Bam saying she should be ready for him. Momma lied and said she had to send Bam away for a spell and he could pick another one. Belinda swallowed and took a step backwards. Everybody looked at the ground hoping he didn't pick them. I was disgusted seeing him literally drool as his eyes went from sister to sister. When he got to me his eyes twinkled, he pointed to me and told my momma he wanted *that one*. Like I was a piece of meat on display at the butcher's counter. My momma told him to have me back before my daddy came home. Slick wiped his drool and he led me by my arm to the car. My sisters and momma watched in silence. Slick laughed to his self as he started the car. He kept telling me I was real pretty and he was going to be gentle cause he wanted me to like it. I didn't know what he meant, I was scared, and I wanted to be anywhere but with him. He took us in the hills of Oakland where no one was around and then he told me to get in the back. He took something out of his wallet and opened the wrapper that kind of looked like a lollipop wrapper with his teeth. I stared at the ceiling of the car as this disgusting man drooled all over me and hurt me. I cried all the way home. Momma met me at the car and she put her arms around me. I cried on her shoulder as Slick told my momma I was good and I wiggled like a fish. She told him to shut up and then she took me to the bathroom. She made a bath and she put salt in the water. She told me to sit. She told me to tell her everything that happened from the moment I got in the car. She asked me if he gave me any money. When I said no then she got mad, she searched my dress as if I would've lied to her. Then she stormed out, I could hear her fussing to somebody outside the bathroom. She told me to get out the tub. I came out in my towel and Macio was standing there with murder in his eyes. "You ok sis?" I shook my head no as I stared at the ground. "He's dead!" Macio said storming out the door.

Momma looked at me, "I don't know who Slick thinks he is. You all too pretty for him to think he ain't giving me nothing!" She sighed, "go put something on. Fix your face before your daddy come home."

I went in the room Tricey and my other sister Lon looked at me with no sympathy. "Welcome to the club, now you're another one of her hoes."

I plopped on the bed. I got dressed then we heard momma talking all sweet to somebody. When I walked out into the living room he was standing in the middle of the floor next to Belinda. He was a man and fine as all get out. He was almost smiling as he looked down at my momma. Belinda looked nervous as they were talking. "Belle who's this?" Lon asked looking him up and down.

"My boyfriend." She looked at momma in fear.

Momma's smile was evil, "how old are you? She's only sixteen."

"I'm nineteen ma'am."

"You got a job?"

"Yes ma'am."

"As you can see our house is full of people. We don't need another mouth to feed."

He looked around the room, "I can see that."

"I'm not signing for you to get married. You're too young! I guess you two will have to figure something else out."

"But momma we're in love!" Belinda cried.

"We'll see how in love you are when your daddy gets here."

Belinda looked at the guy with fear in her eyes, "you should go."

He ignored her, "she's not staying here." He said to momma.

"Who do you think you're talking to? You have no idea who I am!"

"I know exactly who you are. You pimp out the dock walkers. People think it's Slick, Lenny, and them. But I know it's you. I know who your husband is too. I know it all and I don't care. You don't know who I am!" His tall stance seemed to grow taller.

Daddy came busting in the door like momma told him to hurry.

Momma started crying saying that the guy threatened her and that he said he was taking Belinda. Daddy looked at the guy for a minute. He asked him what he wanted with Belinda. The guy said, "she's having my baby."

"How you know it's yours?"

"I know," he said watching my daddy's eyes.

"Take her!" Daddy said as he started walking away.

"WHAT?" My momma yelled but we were all thinking the same thing.

The guy took Belinda by the hand and they walked out the door. Momma was screaming at daddy as he walked to their bedroom. I went out on the porch and I watched them get in his car. I couldn't pull back my jealousy. Nobody else got to choose someone. He put Belinda in the car then he looked back at the house. He smiled at me and said hi as he walked around the car. Lon and Tricey came out too. We watched the car drive away. Lon said that Belinda was dumb and she'd be back. I asked her how she knew. Lon said she's seen him before, she said he was a dog and got a few babies already. I asked why momma was so mad. Tricey said momma's always mad if there's no money in it for her.

****

I asked for another pour of whatever it was it was smooth and delicious. The unfriendly guy filled my glass and then he stared like he wanted me to shut up. I took another sip then I continued.

~

There was this guy Archie at my school. He made me feel weird because he looked at me like I was this angel just because I'm pretty. When I would try to act crazy with him he'd tell me to cut it out.

After Macio provided Slick with a reminder that he needed to pay for my time, Slick came a few more times for me. He made sure he paid my momma, and he always made sure he covered up before he got me. I wanted to be like Belinda and choose for once who would be between my legs. Archie seemed nice enough, so I asked him for a ride one day after school. He asked me where I needed to go. When he started driving I told him anywhere but home. He looked at me for a minute and then he drove. He took me to this little beach outside of a tunnel in Richmond. He looked at me and said now what. I didn't want to stay in the car so I suggested that we walk around. Archie kept looking at me and smiling. Around him I didn't feel dirty or disposable. He made me feel beautiful without saying anything. It's the way he looks at me. He asked me what I wanted to do after high school and I didn't have a clue. He asked me if I wanted to get married and then he laughed. I didn't say anything I just smiled at him. He stared at me and told me I was so pretty again. I took his hand and pulled him into me. I kissed him and that was a wrap. We had sex on the beach in the afternoon almost evening. I liked it; I liked this so much better than that nasty stinky gross man. Every time I thought about going home my heart sped up. I asked Archie to take me to the gas station and I washed up in the bathroom. I knew my momma was gonna get me for not coming straight home but I didn't care. No matter how badly she beat me it wasn't gonna change this experience for me. I made Archie let me out two blocks away from my house. When I got home Belinda was on the couch crying with her baby in her arms. Momma asked me where I've been then JJ came busting in the door. He asked Belinda where her boyfriend was. She said she didn't know. Momma rubbed Belinda's back; "this is why you don't put no man before your family. You over there playing house and he's falling for somebody else. Look at how pretty this baby is. You sure it's a boy? He's so pretty. What's his name?"

"Leonard."

Momma smiled, "you call him after my brother? He just got prettier."

"Why you ain't bring him around?" I was jealous and I don't know why.

"For what? Momma the only one who cared to come see him. None of you guys even checked on me while I was pregnant. I didn't run away like Bam did."

"You trying to come back or something? Cause there's no room for you. Lon sleep in your bed now."

Momma smiled at me then she asked Belinda what she was going to do. She said she was going to spend the night on the couch.

The next morning as I closed the door to leave for school, Belinda's boyfriend was pulling up to the house. He stood up out the car, "is she sleep?"

"YEP." I looked at him.

"Wake her up." He was impatient.

"Can't, gotta go to school." I started to walk.

I could feel his eyes on me. "You need a ride?"

"If you're offering yes."

He waved me on as he got back in his car. I tried to hold back my excitement. "How many of you all are there?"

I looked back at the house and my momma was watching from the window. I sat in the front seat, "sometimes I don't know."

"One of your sisters goes with my boy."

"Which one?"

"Heck if I know, I can't say the pretty one cause that's all of you." I smiled cause that included me. "You dating yet?"

"A little," I couldn't pull back my smile.

He looked at me, and then he looked me up and down. "You look hungry."

"You gonna feed me?"

He squinted his eyes at me, "don't play with me. I'll pull this car over and feed you alright."

"You'd do that to my sister?"

"Like you care."

I didn't say anything to that cause I didn't. When we pulled up to the school I scooted over to him. I pressed my body against his. I kissed his neck while my hand went between his legs. I whispered thank you for the ride in his ear. He didn't react, and then I walked in the school feeling good about myself.

When I got home my momma called me into her room. She asked me why Belinda's boyfriend gave me a ride this morning, I shrugged. Then momma asked me if I knew how to give head. I had no idea of what she was talking about. With the use of a banana she explained everything. She showed me how to rub it to bring him back. She showed me where to hold it to stop him from exploding. She told me to use condoms so I wouldn't get pregnant. She said there were too many babies as it stands. I asked her why she was showing me all of this while she put condoms in my hand. She said she's had the same conversation with my sisters but they don't listen. She said Belinda went around her so she's not telling her nothing. She said Belinda could never handle a man like hers without momma's help. Momma said she was going to wait for Belinda to come home crying again.

****

Life was good Slick was in jail and even though he thought my momma had me at home waiting on him I was sneaking away with Archie practicing everything momma showed me. Archie has asked me to marry him so many times that it's becoming our running joke. Meanwhile I can't stop thinking about Belle's man. Even though every time she comes over we end up fighting cause momma told her that her man gave me a ride to school that time. She says I'm always wanting what belongs to others. So I tease her and tell her how good her man tastes. She gets so mad, even though she knows I haven't had her man. Melanie told her I was at school early that morning cause she saw us pull up.

Melanie quietly sits over to the side never saying much. Momma says Melanie has no heart cause she's always trying to make things better. I think momma gets her just because she's weak.

When I went to the bathroom one night Melanie was in the living room crying as quietly as she could. It didn't sound like she was mad more like her heart was broken. I asked her what was wrong, Melanie fidgeted for a minute then she cried some more. She said she was pregnant. I told her I didn't know momma put her out. Her eyes pleaded with me as she said momma didn't. She said she thought he loved her. She said he promised to always love her, and as soon as she told him she was pregnant he ran away. I asked her if she was the one going with Belle's man's friend. She shook her

26

head yes. I asked her when she was going to tell momma. I felt bad for her cause she was as weak as momma says she is. I don't know why she would believe some guy. Melanie said she couldn't tell momma. It's not like her man was paying for anything. She said momma would try to make her lose the baby. I told her she better get fat like yesterday to try to hide it as long as she could. Melanie begged me not to tell momma on her. She said she couldn't trust anybody and she had to tell somebody.

Over the months I kept asking myself why I was helping her. Honestly Melanie's never done anything to me but be nice to me. I even had her sleep in my bed closest to the wall so her secret wouldn't be discovered at night. Momma told her she was going to put her on a diet cause she was getting too fat.

We were walking to school and Melanie was tired and moving slow when she looked at me funny. The ground under her skirt started getting wet. I told her to stop peeing, and she said she wasn't. Melanie grabbed her stomach as she slowly started falling. A car pulled over and Melanie's teacher Ms. Rieble got out the car and came running. Ms. Rieble hates me and most of us, but she loves Melanie. We got in her car and she took us to the hospital. Melanie kept saying her stomach hurt. They took Melanie in the back and I paced in the waiting room. Momma was gonna get her, but at least her baby would be here and safe right? The principal and vice principal came to the hospital. Everyone was making such a fuss over Melanie. Momma came while the principal was telling me how they were going to figure out how to help her. Everyone was talking almost at once praising Melanie for being such a sweet young lady. The nurse came out and said Melanie had a healthy baby boy. Everyone looked shocked, the vice principal gasped. They looked at the fire in momma's eyes. Ms. Rieble jumped up, "SHE WAS RAPED!" Everybody looked at this teacher who was desperate to protect one of her beloved students from the wrath of her momma. Ms. Rieble made up this whole story that everyone except my momma bought. The principal and vice principal started coming up with a plan on the spot to help Melanie. Momma started calming when they mentioned financial support. I snuck to the recovery room and I told Melanie as fast as I could all the stuff that developed in the waiting room. Then all the adults came in the room. Momma asked Melanie kindly why she didn't come to her. Melanie said she was scared. Everyone told her she was a victim and she shouldn't fear anyone. It seemed like Ms. Rieble even convinced herself that she was telling the truth. When Melanie said she named the baby Troy I asked her what kind of a name was that? Ms. Rieble got so excited as she exclaimed **Helen of *Troy***. My momma flashed me a look cause that lady seemed crazy. Ms. Rieble said she'd be back tomorrow. When they left momma slapped Melanie hard, then she pointed to her armband where it clearly said "Melanie Davis". Momma asked where was the guy. Melanie cried and said she didn't know. Momma asked her how she marry him and then not know where he went. Then momma picked up the baby and looked at his face. She said he was special and then she told her she did good.

****

Link and Leroy were talking on the porch. I was bored so I went out to them. "Where you going? Can I go?"

"Go with us?" They scoffed at me.

Momma's voice surprised us, "that's not a bad idea. Take her with you. Make sure you meet somebody good."

"I'm not her pimp, what am I supposed to do with her?"

"Ain't nobody asked a fool who can't count to pimp nobody! Just take your sister with you!"

Tricey, Jan, and Lon came running, "we want to go too!"

I sucked my teeth cause now it was going to be a family affair. Melanie was in charge of watching all the kids and then even momma decided she was going. Everybody piled into cars and we went to my daddy's spot. I guess this unusually warm late winter almost spring night brought everyone out. Momma looked around at all of the nice cars and I swore I saw dollars signs in her eyes. She told my brothers to go on and then she wanted to look her girls over. She fixed our hair looked at our dresses. I have to admit we all looked pretty, but looking for the highest bidder wasn't what I had in mind for tonight. I wanted to relax. Momma told us to look for her from time to time. I don't know what they used to use this warehouse for but daddy had it fixed up really nice. There was a section for all the fights, and upstairs were all the gambling tables, music, and liquor. Most guys came alone or with their mistresses. I did a couple laps around the place watching heads turn as I walked around. Then I spotted him as he was looking at me. He was an older man and black as the night. It was something about this man that held on to my attention and I found myself approaching him. I couldn't tell if he wanted me by the look of him, his eyes didn't give him away like most guys. "Good evening sir."

"Good evening."

"Are you alone? I don't want your old lady getting mad at me." I smiled, he didn't.

"You are a little girl, who would be upset about a little girl?"

"I'm not completely little."

"To me you are." Then his eyes went back to his cards.

Momma came up to the table, she looked at the man then she looked at me. "What's the game?"

"Bid whist," the other guy at the table said.

"Every man for himself? You've only got three players."

"You gonna sit down?" The other guy at the table asked.

"Partner how high you wanna go?"

He looked her up and down, "Fifty dollars."

"Fifty dollars?" Momma said like he offended her, as if that was no money.

"Let's see if you're any good first."

Momma winked at me, "fine." She threw in twenty-five in chips.

My friend and his partner put in a hundred. Momma said she had four books high in clubs. Her partner said one. Momma started trash talking immediately. No thanks to her partner she made her books and then immediately she was calling for a new partner, she said she needed someone who knew how to play the game cause her last partner was going to get a Boston run on them. Lon came over and volunteered to play as momma's partner. My friend looked at Lon then he looked at me. Then he looked at momma for a minute, he shook his head and then he went back to his hand. Momma and Lon played really well, but my friend still won. Momma raised the stakes on the game. They lost again, and then she suggested raising the stakes again. My friend laughed and then his deep voice rumbled the table. "You can't hustle me, cut to the chase. How much you want?"

"Seventy-five for the night."

"What makes you think I need to pay for company?"

"I'm sure you don't need to, but you came here alone. I think you need company that knows how to leave when it's time." Then she smiled, "which one you want?"

He looked at me, "even the baby?" He shook his head as he adjusted in his seat.

"Oh well you're not interested. How about you?" She asked his partner who had been watching me all night.

My friend dropped one hundred in chips on the table. "For both."

"Both?" Momma shook her head, "no."

"That one is too little, but she has a certain freshness to her." Then he threw twenty-five more in chips on the table. "Ladies lets go."

"Pleasure doing business with you." Momma said smiling as she picked up her chips. Then she looked at my friend's partner. "I have more if you're interested."

"What's you're name suga?" Lon said popping her gum.

"No! Go spit the gum out!" He commanded Lon. She looked surprised and then she did as she was told. When she came back he looked from Lon to me. "Ready?"

"Mister, you still haven't told us your name."

"Call me Whispers."

"That's your birth name?"

"Pretty much, what are your names?"

"I'm Lon and this is my little sister Pam."

"Why your momma got her out here like she grown?"

Lon shrugged, "she start us all out young."

He looked Lon up and down, "then you should be a real pro by now."

"I guess." Lon looked around, "where are we?"

"Hotel, wait here." He got out the car.

"He would be real fine if he wasn't so black!" She took a deep breath, "I can do this!"

"You nervous?"

"Aren't you?" She eyed me.

"Normally I am, but he don't make me nervous."

Lon exhaled, "must be nice."

Whispers came back to the car and parked then he told us to come on. We walked behind him into this place so fancy, I couldn't stop looking around. I gasped really loud when we stepped in the room. He ordered food and then he asked us if we were hungry. Lon and I pretended that it didn't matter, but I know I hadn't eaten since the little bit of cereal I had for breakfast. The guy brought two burgers and a dinner plate. Whispers ate quietly while he watched us devour our burgers and fries. Once the smell of the burger hit my nose I was too hungry to fake it. This was the best burger I've ever had in my life. Lon got up and started to walk towards Whispers. He told her to go take a bath. Lon put her hand on her hip and said she was clean. Whispers told her she also sat around for the last so many hours and then he told her to go get in the bath. Lon frowned, but she did as she was told. Then he looked at me, he told me to follow him into the bedroom. He turned on the television and I got so excited cause it was a color television. He told me I was sleeping in the bedroom with him. I asked him if he wanted me to get in when Lon got out. He told me I could take a shower but I needed to put something on when I came out. Then he called down to the front desk. He told them he needed a t-shirt and a pair of men's boxers. He said I could sleep in that. I didn't get it, but I said ok. Lon got out the bathtub she brought the t-shirt and boxers in the room to me. She had on a white robe. She told me to feel it. It was soft and lush. Then she told me to smell the lotion, and it smelled really good. She said I was going to love the tub. I got in the shower like he told me to. I had so much fun washing myself with this really good soap. It smelled delicious. When I came out of the bathroom Lon was on her knees and Whisper's back was to me in a chair. I quickly went to the room and I shut the door. I still had on the extremely soft robe over my t-shirt and shorts. I felt like I was a royal princess in this robe. All about Eve was on and I couldn't take my eyes off of the movie. It was so good! I know I was supposed to learn a lesson from all of that, but all I could focus on was how Eve came in and took over. I heard the shower, and then I cracked the door to see who was in the bathroom. Lon was naked and knocked out in the middle of the pullout bed in there. The sheet barely covered her. I got a little nervous and then I told myself to suck it up. I got under the covers in the bed and I waited. When Whispers came in the room the first thing I noticed was how muscular his thighs were. He had on boxers and no shirt. He had his clothes neatly folded in his hands and he set them on the chair. "If you steal from me, I will hurt you." How could I ignore such a direct threat? He got on the bed and laid on top of the covers that I was under. He told me to turn the TV and light off. I did as I was told and then I got back under all the covers. Even when my eyes adjusted to the darkness I couldn't see Whispers in the dark. I asked him what his real name was, and he told me to never mind that. His strong hand touched me and I held my breath, when he put his arm around me I exhaled. That night was interesting and I woke up confused. I wondered if he slept at all, cause at one point he went back out to Lon. At first I thought she was faking, but then I realized she couldn't fake what I was hearing. I laid still like I was sleep when he came back after he showered again. Then he put his arm around me again. In the morning we got dressed and he took us out to eat, Lon was quiet during breakfast but she kept looking at him funny. I think she likes him and she doesn't normally like anybody. When he dropped us off at home momma asked how everything went and we said fine. She asked us if he gave us any more money. Lon said he probably gave her everything he had last night. Momma agreed then she went out the door with Macio as he rallied the little ones for training. Lon pulled me in the room. "Did you do it?"

"What do you mean?"

"I never heard you."

"I didn't know I was supposed to be as loud as you were."

She swallowed like she was remembering something that tasted delicious. "I wasn't trying to be that loud." I smiled, "so you did?"

"Why are you all up in my business?" I yanked my arm away from her.

"He's weird." I could see it in her eyes she liked him.

It made me mad, I saw him first. I liked him from the beginning, and she was the one talking about he was too dark. "No he's not, he's a gentleman. Maybe you're just not used to being treated like that."

"Stand down Pam! I'm warning you!"

"He picked me in case you forgot. As long as he picks me I'm going."

Chapter 3

The unfriendly guy frowned at me. "Did you sleep with him?"

I smiled at the fact that I now had his attention and he wanted to know the answer to what I left unsaid on purpose. "Hold on, I'll get to that in a moment." I thought for a minute.

~

And so then, my fascination with him began. I wanted to know where Whispers came from. Who was he? Is Whispers his real name? He's always nicer to me than he is to my sisters, why? He started sending my sisters home and then he'd take me out to eat in the morning, it seemed like he enjoyed watching me enjoy my meal. He was never really a big talker, but I would enjoy whenever he'd grace my ears with anything he had to say. I tried to act like this was normal behavior for me, being treated like somebody special. Normally I would've lied and stuck to my lie when Whispers asked me if he was the first person to ever take me out to eat. Something about the way he looked at me made me tell the truth. Each time I see him I ask at least five times what his real name is. He looks at me like it irritates him but he doesn't respond.

****

Belinda came over in tears AGAIN! I swear if she knew how to please him she wouldn't have so many problems. This time she was crying saying he asked her if the baby was really his. She said she had only ever been with him and she was hurt that he would ask her that. One time I asked Melanie why Belle didn't lie about her age to get married like Melanie did. She said her man wouldn't let her lie. I laughed cause all that said to me is that he knew my parents weren't going to allow it. I wondered why he let her stay with him at all. Did he really care about her? Archie says he loves me, but let me act like I don't feel like giving him some and he acts down right ugly. I wonder if Belle's man acts like that with her. I wonder if he's even any good. It's not like she would know the difference.

****

Friday and Saturday nights have now been hot nights. We get dressed up really nice and then we go down to daddy's spot. Momma even gets into it and dresses up really nice and we have a good time. Sometimes Whispers is there, and whenever he sees me, he watches me. I now know that by the time I see him, he's already seen me and I need to come stand by him. When I didn't understand in the beginning he seemed like he got mad. He doesn't like when other men look at me or anything. He says I'm too young to be out like my momma has me out there. A few times Jan came with us instead of Lon. He got really mad at Jan though cause she was mad that I got to sleep with him in the bed. She tried to fight me in front of him and he wasn't having it. Lon gets smart with him, but she does whatever he tells her to do. I think she sneaks out to see him without momma knowing too. I think she's in love with him, but I can't blame her for loving him. Even though he's black and mean looking he has a way about him that you forget about all of that and you just want to hold him.

I didn't see Whispers' car in the parking lot, so that meant he wasn't coming tonight. I was a little disappointed, cause I was looking forward to being treated delicately. The craps table was hot and everybody was up there making a lot of noise. Some body was on a roll and making a big fuss about it. My sisters and momma were sprinkled through out the crowd and I made my way towards the front to see who it was. This man with a whole group of people kept making a bunch of noise as he threw his dice. They kept making so much noise cause he kept winning. I was going to walk away when I saw him. A young guy was standing next to the winner; he was smiling and taking everything in. He was out with his father and I guess his father was showing him how things were done. The guy was smiling and cheering then he saw me. I smiled at him and he smiled back. When his father realized he was distracted he looked around until he saw me. He smiled and said something to his son. I walked away and continued walking around. It seemed like most people knew that I normally left with Whispers so they weren't paying me much attention. I was standing by the door to get some air when the young guy approached me. "What's your name?"

"Pam."

"I'm Lucas, nice to meet you." I smiled, "what are you doing here?"

"Just walking around meeting people. You from Oakland?" I asked.

"No, we live in the city. My dad heard about this place and we came to check it out."

"And who do we have here?" Momma said, I didn't even see her coming.

"His name is Lucas."

"Aren't you a bit young to be here?" Momma said all sweet.

"I'm here with my dad."

"I'm Momma Shuga, how can I help you?"

"Help me?"

"You looking for company?" She smiled.

His eyes darted to me, "company?"

"It's ok baby, everybody comes here looking for a good time.

Ain't no shame in that."

"You're speaking for her?" Suddenly I felt embarrassed. Normally the men knew exactly what was happening here, but Lucas seemed like he was catching on. It didn't make me feel good about myself.

"Yep, when you decide what you want come talk to me." Then she looked at me, "come on Pam." I followed my momma away feeling horrible.

Lucas watched us walk away then he went back to his group of people. I tried to walk the other way whenever I saw him after that. Then I saw his father talking to my momma. He gave her some chips and she smiled. She came to me and said the little boy was waiting by the door. She looked me in my eyes and said not to let him drive off with me. I swallowed air and then I went to the door. Lucas was standing there with car keys in his hand. He walked and I followed, he opened a car door. I exhaled; I hate being in cars it makes me think of Slick. I stood still, "what?"

"Do we have to get in?"

"I don't understand." He looked confused.

"I don't like cars."

He looked around, "so then what?"

"What do you want me to do?"

"What do you do?" He asked.

"Everything, is this your first time?"

"Sort of…" now he looked embarrassed.

I took his sort of to be a yes. "You know we don't have to lay down to do it right?"

I told him to sit in the doorway of the front seat. I unfastened his belt and I kissed him until he was at attention. His hands were all in my hair as he moaned in pleasure. I took a condom out of my bra and I put it on him. I told him to stand up, as I got ready for him. I bent over against the car a little and then I told him to come up behind me. I guided him in with my hand. He moaned loudly, instinct took over and he was going. He felt good, nothing will ever be as bad as Slick. He even got me going a little when he finished. I fixed my clothes and I told him he was a man now. Lucas looked like he was dizzy for a minute. Since I was now dirty, I went and got in momma's car. Lon was already in the car sleeping. As I started to fall asleep Lucas tapped on the window. Lon opened one eye and she told me to get rid of him. I got out the car and I asked him what was wrong. He asked me why I walked away like that. I told him we were done, he looked irritated. He asked me to go for a ride with him and I told him I couldn't. I told him to come back next week, he could ask my momma for permission to take me for a ride. He didn't look happy but oh well.

The next week he was there and waiting by the door. He and momma went back and forth for a while. His father came over then JJ joined my momma. Then Lucas came over and told me we were leaving, momma told him to bring me back here when he was done. This time he was in a van, and he had blankets and a pillow. I only brought three condoms and he got mad when I said we couldn't go again without one. I told him he didn't want babies running around Oakland that he didn't know about. When he looked disappointed I found myself telling him to back up when he thought it was time and not to release inside of me. I didn't expect it to be good to me too. I got so caught up that when he pulled back I almost told him not to. I told him he was a fast learner and he was ready. Lucas kept kissing on me as he told me I was the real thing. Hearing him say that made me feel weird. Suddenly I wanted to be the real thing to somebody. I guess I hadn't thought of it before. Lucas spent the next I don't know how long kissing me. At first I was letting him kiss me, but when he kept going and going I finally kissed him back. When I kissed him back Lucas started moaning again. He wanted to go but his body wasn't listening to him. That didn't stop him from humping on me as if there was anything he could do. I had to make him take me back to the waterfront. He didn't want to take me. When he parked the van he was going to say something when JJ snatched him out the door. Momma said he owed her more money cause his father only paid for two hours and we were gone for four. When I tried to tell momma it was my fault she started beating on me and telling me to shut up. Macio brought Lucas' father out. Macio calmly explained that they owed my momma more money and they weren't leaving until she got it. Lucas' dad said he already over paid momma as it was and he wasn't paying more. JJ hit Lucas so hard his body slammed into the van denting it. I screamed and I begged JJ not to hurt Lucas. I said it was my fault. Momma punched me in the face and she told me to shut up. Then she told Leroy to put me in the car. Leroy grabbed me by my arm and he drug me to the car calling me a traitor for going against momma. When we were almost to the car a bunch of guys started rushing out of the warehouse. Leroy told me to get in the car then he ran back to momma. I stood next to the car debating on whether I should go back or not. When I saw Whispers come out I ducked and ran to the other side of the car. Lon pointed at momma's car and he was coming. I sucked my teeth, I was already dirty. What is she doing? Whispers came over, grabbed me, and made me go with him with Lon in tow. He put us in his car as I saw people fighting. He didn't take us to the usual hotel; we went over the bridge and to a different hotel in the city. He took us to his room, he told us to clean up then he left. Lon was mad at me but she was waiting for Whispers to leave. She waited and then she opened the door and looked out in the hallway. Then she shut the door. Lon turned to me with fire in her eyes. She ran up and slapped me as hard as she could. She accused me of playing games. She asked me why I would take another trick when I knew Whispers was waiting for me. She said with this fight daddy wasn't going to let us come back down to the waterfront, and then momma was going to put us back on her pimps. Lon was shaking she was so mad. She said she wasn't going back to those nasty dirty men. I wanted to tell her that it wasn't my fault and that momma sent me with Lucas knowing Whispers was there. Didn't matter what I said she was going to be mad. We fought all over that room for a while, but she didn't dare draw blood on me knowing Whispers was coming back. She ran in the bathroom and bathed, and then I showered. I sat in my robe until Whispers brought my T-shirt and shorts like usual. When I heard Lon crying I peeked out the door. Whispers was talking and she was upset. I got in the bed and covered my head. When Whispers came in the room he asked me how long before I turned eighteen. I told him I had a whole year. He seemed irritated by the thought. He asked me if I wanted to move to the city when I turned eighteen. I told him I hadn't thought of what I was going to do. He gently but firmly grabbed my wrist as he told me that I couldn't spend the rest of my life like this. He told me I needed to graduate. None of my sisters graduated, Macio and JJ were the only ones who did. Whispers kissed my forehead and he told me I deserved better.

****

Daddy told momma we couldn't come to the waterfront anymore. Momma was so mad cause she was making a lot of money having us down there. She beat me for not being in the car like she told me to be. Then all my sisters came after me when she told them it was all my fault that we couldn't go back. Like I said we don't fight like we're family, and my sisters didn't go easy on me. I was restricted to the house until my face healed up. Melanie didn't go out much, she normally took care of the kids, and so I found myself spending a lot of time with her. Momma saw us getting close and then she told Melanie that I said all these things that I didn't say. It made me mad that Melanie believed momma. So Melanie and I had a big ole fight around the house until we both backed down. Not too long after that Melanie talked to a social worker about getting on welfare and getting her own place. Momma didn't care if she left, cause she never made money off her anyways. Whenever Belinda would hint around wanting to come home momma would tell her she'd have to bring in money. Belinda would back pedal. Macio tells both of them that regardless of where they're living Belle needed to bring her boy and as soon as Melanie's was walking good she need to bring him for training.

****

So today it's Fuzzy and me. Bam still hasn't come back yet, and Slick acted a fool when I refused him. I'm sorry but I hate that nasty old man. I provoked him to going off so bad that Macio almost killed him for acting like he was going to raise up at momma. I explained to him that I was too pretty for her to be giving me away to that nasty old man. He's not that old, but he's old enough. Slick was acting so bad that it depressed little Fuzzy. My nephew is the only one to show real concern about me so when momma's not looking I sneak him hugs. This morning I told him to meet me on the corner and we'd go anywhere he wanted. We decided to wander to the mall and wander around there. Then I spotted him walking around with a girl. My heart started pounding he's so fine, and he knows it. He didn't even look like he was trying not to get caught with another woman. I stood there looking at Belle's man. He nodded at me and then he walked away. Fuzzy had just picked this man's pocket for money for lunch. Belle's man walked up and asked us what we were doing. Both of us straightened up and said nothing. He told Fuzzy to return it, when Fuzzy tried to play dumb he told him to return the wallet or else he was blowing the whistle on us. Fuzzy told the man he dropped his wallet as he handed it to him. I asked Belle's man what his name was and he squinted his eyes at me and looked away. "Belle's man, we're hungry. Can you buy us something to eat?"

He smiled, "what's in it for me?"

"Feed us and then I'll go where ever you want to go."

He looked at Fuzzy, "you cool little man?"

Fuzzy shrugged, "depends on what I eat."

"What do you want to eat?"

"Buck's Big Burger! I want the onion rings, and a big malt shake."

"What you know about Buck's?"

"Only that I never had it."

"Let's go."

He took us to Buck's and then he told us to order whatever we wanted. He only drank a soda, but we ate good. Buck's was as good as everyone said it was. Some people call it a greasy spoon, I don't care it was delicious. He took us to an apartment complex, he told Fuzzy to go play and I would come get him. I asked him where my sister was and he said she didn't live here. The apartment wasn't fancy and there was a bed in the bedroom, other than that it was pretty empty. I stood by the door. "Come here."

His simple request ignited fire in me. I shook my head no, "I don't even know your name."

"You know the names of all the tricks you turn?"

I wanted to run out the door. I dropped my head. "Is that what this is?"

"This ain't no love connection." He stood in the middle of the floor.

I got mad, "fine. We discuss price first and you need a condom. This is not how I envisioned spending my afternoon."

He smiled, "I hurt your feelings?"

"Doesn't matter, make me an offer."

He reached in his pocket. He pulled out a wad of money. "Will this cover you?"

I walked up to him and took the money. I started counting when he grabbed my hand then he pulled me in to kiss him. His kiss was even better than Lucas' kiss. We moved into the room he undid his pants then he sat on the bed. He pushed my head like he was anxious. I smiled at him, "you gotta tell me your name first."

He squinted his eyes at me, that squint seemed familiar but I didn't pay it much attention. "Stop playing!" I folded my arms and looked at him. "Fine! It's Eugene!"

I smiled at him and proceeded to pullout all the stops. I am good at what I do if I have nothing else going for me. Eugene's uncontrolled moans were confirmation that my sister was not on her job. When we were done I laid there trying to catch my breath. Eugene looked at me and said he wasn't expecting all that. He said my sister won't do any of the things we did. He said it's a lot of work for him to get in. I could totally see my sister trying to play the good girl. To say he was satisfied would be an understatement. He got excited when he realized he had one more condom. I had him calling out my name. I knew I was in trouble when I called out his.

****

Eugene told me not to tell my momma about me and him. I do whatever he tells me to. If he tells me to stay at the apartment I stay even though I know that means she's going to get me when I come home. Everything with Eugene is worth any beating my momma could do. Cuts and bruises heal, but going without Eugene seems to be more than I can bare. I hide my money outside before I come in the house. If momma thought I was holding out on her it would mean a world of hurt for me.

I laugh at him every time he says that this time is the last time. By the time I'm done with him he's begging me to spend the night. He said he wasn't going to keep the apartment, but now he's bought the things I need so that I can stay there from time to time.

Every time I come home and Belinda is there she looks at me like she's looking for the answer to something. "Your momma still be trying to put you out?" Eugene asked as he ran his hand over my body.

"YEP! That's why she keeps beating on me cause I don't want to go."

"What if you stay here?"

"You said this wasn't no love connection." I tried to pull back my excitement.

"I don't love you, but your stuff is so good I get confused. I don't care if they're paying, I'm greedy and I want your stuff all for me."

"What about my sister?"

"What about her?"

"She's in love with you."

"I'm in love with her, but the good girl routine gets old. Besides I know she's trying to leave me."

"Is she really that dumb?"

He smiled at me, "that would be dumb of her wouldn't it?"

I got on top of him, "you tired of paying me?"

"I want you here when I want you. Waiting for you to sneak away is nerve racking at times. Besides when I disappear lately she's running over to your parents. She's noticing that we're both missing around the same times. Just stay."

"How am I supposed to get my stuff?"

"Leave it, it's too risky to have you go back."

"Ok, so you're going to pay for me to stay here?"

"Yep, you better not ever bring another man here. And I don't want to hear he's your brother crap either. No men!"

"Any other rules my lord?"

"Do you love me?" He watched my face.

I wanted to lie and say no, but he was watching me. "Um!"

"Go ahead and admit it." He smiled.

Suddenly I thought about Whispers. "Um!"

His smile dropped, "I'm not asking about whoever he is. I'm asking you about me."

"Yes, but you don't love me."

"So! I love what you do. Now.." He grabbed my hips, "do it again."

****

"PAM!" I jumped so hard. I caught the bus all the way over here so that I wouldn't run into anyone I knew and still someone's calling my name like they know me. I turned around and it was Archie.

I smiled, "hey Archie!"

"Where did you go? You disappeared without so much as a goodbye."

"That's the whole point of dropping out. You disappear suddenly."

"How could you do that to me? Nobody knew where you went."

"It wasn't against you. I had to get out of my parent's house."

He smiled, "give me your number."

"I don't have a phone. But give me your number and I'll call you."

"You need a ride?"

"Um," I hesitated. Eugene said no men.

"Please don't tell me you have a boyfriend."

"I do actually, and we live together." I smiled really big.

"PAM! You're breaking my heart! You're supposed to marry me." He put his hand on his chest.

"You weren't serious!"

"Yes I am! I guess I'm waiting for you to realize it."

"Yeah ri...." He pulled me in and kissed me. Has everyone been taking kissing lessons except me?

"PAM!" I jumped again at the sound of my name. I turned around and it was Belle. "Where have you been? Momma's been looking for you!" If I ever thought my sister hated me this moment confirmed it.

I backed away from Archie. "I had to leave."

"She's been going crazy looking for you."

"I bet she has. I know you're going to run back and tell her you saw me. Just tell her I'm ok."

"No, you're coming with me." She reached out to grab me and I hit her hand away.

"I'm not going back there!" Her baby was sitting in the shopping cart watching us. I ran on the opposite side of the cart. When she moved towards me I tipped the cart threatening to throw it over. "Leave me alone Belle!"

"You wouldn't!"

"Wouldn't I!" Then I looked at Archie, "baby please bring the car around."

Archie hurried out the door. The little boy was looking at me looking like a combination of Belle and Eugene. I said hi to him and he said hi back. Belle was trying to think of how to corner me without hurting her little man. I told Belle her kid was cute, then I said he must look like his daddy cause she was the ugly one. She got mad and tried to move the cart. I gripped it for dear life. Archie pulled up by the door, he was waiting with his motor running. With all my might I jerked the cart and pushed it in the opposite direction. Then I grabbed my bags and ran as hard as I could. Belle stopped the cart then she screamed runaway as she ran behind me. I got in Archie's car then I gasped for air. He stood on the gas and took off. When we were a few blocks away he pulled into a residential area and turned the car off. I looked around looking to see if a car followed us. Archie asked me why I ran away from home. I told him my momma didn't like my boyfriend, and I had to be with him. Archie asked what about him, he said he was in love with me. I smiled and touched his chin. I didn't know what else to say or do, so I put my head in his lap.

I had Archie drop me a block away from my apartment. As I was
getting out of the car Eugene stopped in the middle of the street.
He walked over like he was going to hurt Archie. I screamed out
that Archie was just a guy from school and he saved me from
Belle. He paused then he looked at Archie's car like he was making
a mental note. He told him to get out of here. He still grabbed me
by my arm and threw me in his car. When we walked into the
apartment he put my bags on the table then he told me to strip.
When I acted like I wasn't going to do it he grabbed me by my
neck and told me to do it! I took my clothes off and he sniffed over
every part of my body. When his nose got between my legs he
asked me what I got excited about. I said quickly I got excited
when I saw him. He said I looked guilty when he saw me. So I said
it was because of the whole Belle scene. He sat at the table and he
told me to sit on his lap and tell him what happened. I didn't tell
him about the kiss but I told him about everything else. He was
touching me until I got to the part about the baby in the cart. He
grabbed my face and threw me on the floor. He took off his belt
and swung it in the air like he was going to hit me. He told me if I
valued my life I could never hurt Leonard. I didn't say anything
then I heard the belt cut threw the air and it felt like lightning hit
my leg. I screamed then I said ok. He stood there staring at me
while I cried. His face held no sympathy for me. He told me to put
my groceries away, and then he watched me. He sat down at the
table and ran his hand over his face. When I attempted to pick up
my dress, his eyes turned evil and he asked me what I was doing. I
told him I was cold. He pushed me face down over the table and
very roughly took me from behind. He pulled out before he
exploded; he fixed his pants, dropped money on the table, and
walked out the door.

****

Eugene hasn't come back in weeks and I feel horrible. I miss him
so badly; I wasn't going to hurt the baby on purpose. Threatening

him was the only way to get Belle to back down. A couple times I've gone down to the pay phone on the corner and called Archie. We talk until my time runs out.

Tonight I was sitting in the middle of the bed when I heard the front door. My heart leaped for joy. Eugene looked mad when he walked in the room. I froze cause I thought he was still mad at me. He started pacing and then he went off. He said his day started with an argument with his father. He's never mentioned his father so I listened. He said Malcolm acts like he's a little kid who knows nothing. "At work someone called me junior and he seemed to think that was funny. I told him my name was Eugene and I had my own junior. Malcolm says I was over reacting, but the only reason he knows me is because I found him. It's not like he was looking for me."

I asked him if his father knew about him. He deflated as he said no, then he got mad and said that wasn't the point. He said his father could be heartless at times and there were a lot of things about him that were hard to deal with. Then he said he went home and Belle moved out. I tried to hide my excitement. Belle said he takes no interest in their son, and that he didn't even know Eugene. I asked if that was true. He said he's at work before the kid woke up and most times he didn't get home until he was in the bed. Eugene says she's been asking if he ever slept with me. My eyes got big and I asked him why she asked him that. He didn't know, and then he told me to get dressed cause he was taking me out. I got excited and I got out that bed so fast. I ran to the shower and then I fixed my hair. He smiled at me and he told me I looked pretty. We went out with some of his friends; I had such a good time.

****

Even though Eugene and Belle broke up, I was still restricted to this apartment. Eugene took me out sometimes, but I quickly learned that another girl had replaced Belle. I was still his best-kept secret.

I was making dinner when Eugene walked in the door. He was talking to someone so I froze. He never brings anyone here. My heart stopped beating when Whispers walked in the door. Whispers' expression didn't change, but I was stuck. "Pam this is my father." Eugene said not paying me any attention.

My eyes pleaded with him not to say anything. "Hello."

"How do you know her?"

"She's Belle's sister."

"One of Barb's girls?"

"Yes." Eugene walked to the closet not paying his father attention.

Whispers squinted his eyes at me and that's when I realized that Eugene does that just like him. "One of her men just washed up on shore."

"I heard about that. It was one of her pimps."

"Your mother's a pretty vicious woman." Whispers said to me.

"Which one?"

"They called him Slick." He watched me.

"I hated him!"

"Most people did, he's been taken care of."

Eugene took the locked box out the closet, and then he looked at us. "What are you saying?"

"You heard me." Whispers sat on the couch.

Eugene frowned at me then he looked at his father. "How do you know her?"

"Momma Shuga used to bring all her girls down to Tipp's."

"Since when you pay for company?"

"I could ask you the same thing."

Eugene looked at me, "go in the room and shut the door."

I turned off the stove then I did as I was told. I couldn't hear what they were talking about. I always wondered what was in that locked box, but I didn't dare touch it. After awhile I heard the front door and then Eugene opened the door. "Did you screw my father?"

"No!" I said too fast.

He didn't believe me; he stood in the doorway staring at me.

****

It was raining and cold, I was reading a book in the bed when I heard a knock at the door. I thought it was my neighbor coming to *borrow* an egg or a cup of sugar. If it was Eugene he'd use his key. Sound left me as I looked at Whispers standing in front of me. He didn't wait for me to invite him in, he walked in. I said a scared Eugene, and he said that Eugene was on his way to LA for a *candy show*. I asked what that was, and he told me to never mind that. Then he shut the door behind him. I smiled and I told him I knew his name. He didn't smile back all he said was Eugene talked too much.

Whispers stayed for a while then he left. In the morning I asked Archie for a ride to the Laundromat so that I could wash all my clothes and sheets. Archie was all hands as if he never saw Eugene.

He showed me his condom and I told him it was his funeral. Something about all the sneaking made everything better.

Eugene came that evening with a new dress for me. He told me to get dressed cause he was taking me out. He was in a really good mood. Eugene was full of hugs and kisses all the affection I needed from him and have been wanting. We were at some guy I didn't know's house. Eugene kept telling me how pretty I looked, I couldn't stop blushing. He had a little debate with himself and then he asked me if I brought a condom. He looked disappointed when I said no. He debated with himself and then he took my hand and led me up the stairs. He told his friend he'd be right back. His friend laughed and said yea right. The door barely closed before he was all over me. He went in stronger and deeper than before. I was prepared to try to keep my whits about myself and move out the way when it was time, but Eugene roared as he laid in long and strong on my spot. He nutted and then he kept going, then he nutted again, kept going and then the final time my eyes rolled all the way in the back of my head. Eugene collapsed on me then he slowly withdrew. He kissed me and then he said we were doing that again. I asked him why he didn't pull out. He ignored my question and said tonight was just what he needed.

****

He kept looking back at me, and I was trying to keep my distance. I held on to Eugene's arm and I put my head down. I didn't need any problems, and I didn't know what Lucas was going to do. He looked surprised to see me. Eugene asked me who the guy was and I kept my eyes down. Eugene sucked his teeth then he called Lucas over to our table. He invited him to sit down. Eugene sat back and asked Lucas what he could help him with. Lucas said he was trying to see if he knew me. Eugene said he saw me now what did he want. Lucas shook his head and said he didn't know I was here with Eugene. Eugene got mad, he said Lucas saw me sitting with Eugene not talking to anyone else. He told Lucas to go away.

Lucas got mad and said something smart. Eugene moved fast and broke Lucas down right there in front of everybody. Lucas' father and entourage came over thinking Eugene was alone. Eugene stood on Lucas' back and asked his friends to escort Lucas and his people out. Eugene grabbed me by my hair and pulled me towards the back of the building. He told me to get in the car. The whole car ride he called me out of my name in every way he could think of. I cried as I told him I didn't have a choice. I told him my momma made me do it. I told him that he saved me. He got quiet as I poured out everything. I told him that momma gave us away to the highest bidder. I kept talking as we sat in the car. When he reached out to me I thought he was going to hit me and I braced myself. Instead he hugged me and told me it was my fault for being so pretty and good at what I do.

Chapter 4

I walked home from the clinic in a daze. If Eugene tossed Belle to the side and he actually cared about her, then there was no hope for me. Even though he should know this baby is his, what if it wasn't? When I got home I made myself breakfast. I was sitting at the table then Eugene walked in off schedule. He looked angry, I braced myself to be hit because of the way he walked in the door. Eugene stood over me, "why were you at the clinic this morning?"

I knew his friend saw me even though I hoped he didn't. "I'm late!"

Betrayal was all over Eugene's face. "Who's is it?"

"How could you ask me that? You were there! You didn't even pull out!"

"You're lying! Who's is it?"

"It's yours!"

Eugene took a deep breath then he marched out, slamming the door behind him when he left.

****

I gave the paperwork to my caseworker. She watched my face then she asked me how I was doing. One afternoon I broke down at her desk. I didn't want to be anybody's momma. That's why I always made sure everybody else covered up. No matter how strong and carefree I was with everyone else, I was always weak for Eugene and he knew it. The only reason to care about this baby was because of Eugene even though he keeps telling me it's not his baby. But then he does stuff like bring me fruits and vegetables. A couple times he's come in the middle of the night. He got in the bed and rubbed my stomach kissing it when he thought I was sleep.

I told my caseworker I didn't know. She was one of the few people I could show how depressed I am. I called Archie from the pay phone outside of the clinic. When I told him I was pregnant he immediately asked me if the baby was his. When I hesitated he got excited but I couldn't tell over the phone if that was a good excitement or what. He told me he wanted to see me, but I told him my boyfriend has been acting weird and I couldn't. He reluctantly agreed to patiently wait. Meanwhile he gave me the address of his job and told me to come by as soon as I could. I got on the bus to make my way home. Then a chubby woman got on the bus all huffy. I glanced at her and then I looked back out the window. Then it registered who she was and I did a double take. She was staring at me with anger in her eyes. It was Bam! I nervously smiled at her cause I didn't know if she wanted to fight me or not. "What are you doing all the way out here?" She called out across the aisle from me.

"I just came from my caseworker."

She tilted her head, "caseworker?"

"I ran away when I was seventeen."

Her face softened and then she sat in front of me. She turned to face me. "Did you hear? Our father died."

"What? When?"

"All of Oakland is talking about it. I'm surprised no one told you."

I felt something but I couldn't tell you what it was. "Should I be sad?"

"I can't tell you how to feel. You going to go to the funeral?" She asked me.

"Momma will get me."

"You think she still cares?" Her eyes pleaded for me to say no.

"I saw Belle a while back and she was acting like she was going to drag me back there."

"Momma never put her out HUH?"

"No, or Melanie." That irritated me.

"Melanie is weak though."

"She put Slick on me after you left."

Bam's eyes turned evil, then she smiled a little. "He died." She said lowly with a smirk. "It was a painful and horrible death too."

"Last I knew Fuzzy was missing you."

"I don't know why."

"You're his momma."

"I didn't ask for any of those kids. Momma put that nasty man on me." Then she looked at me, "that from one of your tricks?" She pointed to my stomach.

"No, my boyfriend."

She smiled, "who is he?"

"His name is Archie." I couldn't trust her and I wasn't telling a soul about Eugene.

"Never heard of him. Where you going?"

I couldn't say I was going home in case she followed me. "I don't know yet. Where you going?"

"Momma's house, you wanna come?"

"You go over there?"

Fear flashed over her face. "This was going to be my first time. I figure I need to pay my respects and find out when the funeral is."

"Fine!" I heard myself say. At least if she beat me maybe I'd lose this baby.

Bam looked as scared as I did as we walked towards momma's house. There were a bunch of cars; I only focused on Eugene's. Why was he here? I thought Belle left him. The closer we got to the house the louder everyone seemed. Bam's hand was shaking really hard as she reached out to turn the doorknob. She made me walk in first with my stomach sticking out. A hush fell over the room. I looked around at the angry faces of my siblings. Eugene was standing against the wall with his arms around Belle. They didn't look broken up to me. My eyes landed on momma who was sitting on the couch looking the maddest. Bam stood next to me probably feeling the same way I did. "What do you want?" She barked at us.

"Pam and Bam, both of the runaways. I told you they were probably together." Lon said.

"We're not together, she lives with her boyfriend." Bam blurted.

"That guy I saw you kissing on?" Belle asked. If looks could kill, Eugene's stare would've shot me.

"You didn't see me kissing anybody."

"Why lie about it? Nobody here cares who you kiss!" Her eyes burned me.

Momma was looking at Belle and Eugene. "Pam, who's baby is that?"

"My boyfriend's. I didn't come here to get asked a bunch of questions. I wanted to know when the funeral is."

"Why? You didn't care about your father." Momma said.

"I cared about him as much as he cared about me."

That made momma mad and she got up and in my face. "For all you know he died cause he was worried about you." When I looked at Bam, her eyes were on Fuzzy and Renee. Both of them were staring at her with hatred in their eyes. Momma pushed me backwards and I almost fell.

"Barb!" Eugene's voice roared. "Don't do her like that, she's pregnant."

"Why would you care what I do to my daughter?"

"Cause she's pregnant."

"Since when you care about babies? Your son is in the other room and he don't even know who you are. Mind your own business." Momma said coming for me.

Eugene grabbed momma's hand. "Barb! Stop!"

"Take your hands off my momma!" JJ said stepping forward.

"Tell your momma to calm down!" Eugene stood tall waiting for JJ to do something.

"I'm not telling my momma nothing." JJ moved closer. "You need to...."

"Eugene! You're gonna fight my brother over PAM?" Belle was mad.

"Your sister is pregnant. Why would she touch her?"

"Cause she's a selfish liar. Don't defend her!"

"Her baby don't deserve this."

"Don't nobody care about her bastard! Like my momma said if you wanna be concerned about a kid our son is out back. He don't even know what you look like."

"Pam, are you messing around with Belle's man?" Lon asked with a smile.

Belle got mad, "who's baby is that?"

"My boyfriend's, you saw him."

"If he's your man why would you deny kissing him?" She was closing in on me.

"Belinda! Stop it! Your momma got all you guys turning on each other and you don't even know why. Nor are you smart enough to ask why."

"I bet that's Whispers' baby." Lon volunteered.

Eugene's eyes darted to me. "It's not, I've never slept with Whispers."

Momma started laughing, "right! He was coming out the pocket to spend time with you and you weren't spreading for him? Yea right! You still see him don't you?"

"Momma! No!"

"Why are you here?" Fuzzy barked at his momma.

"My father died."

"You don't care!" Fuzzy said.

"You've got a lot of nerve showing up here after all these years." Lon yelled.

"He was my father!" Bam yelled.

"You're my momma! You gonna show up when I die looking for sympathy?"

Bam turned and walked out the door. I walked out behind her. When my foot hit the last step I heard the commotion from inside. Momma came flying out the door. I grabbed my stomach and ran a few steps. She jumped on Bam; she told her that she was the reason I ran away. Eugene was telling Belle to come on, and she was arguing with him. He threw his hands at Belle then he told my momma to stop hitting Bam. He caught momma's hand and JJ came charging. Eugene spun momma to make her stop then he readied himself for JJ. JJ was trying to size Eugene up, Eugene wasn't scared and he was calm. Leroy came out to join JJ and my heart felt like it stopped beating. My brothers are mean and vicious. Momma was cursing Eugene she called him all kinds of stupids and she told him he brought this on himself. JJ moved in to hit Eugene and some how he just missed his face. Eugene grabbed his arm and picked big ole JJ up and threw him into Leroy, which made both of them fall. Eugene put his knees in JJ's back and stayed on Leroy's face. Leroy's body went limp and then Eugene got up. JJ got up fast promising death to Eugene. Personally after he picked me up like I was nothing I would've backed down. But I guess since my entire family was watching he had to go out fighting. When Eugene hit JJ you heard it and then his body spun around and he fell. Eugene told Bam and I to get in his car. Momma was standing there looking with big eyes like she couldn't believe anyone could beat her big ole boys. Bam got in the front crying holding her face. Eugene asked Bam where she lived and then we dropped her off. When Bam got out the car Eugene went off on me asking me why I went back there when I knew no one there loved me. I asked him why he didn't tell me my father died.

He said it didn't matter cause my father was never a real father to me. I cried then he backhanded me so hard everything went silent and I grabbed my nose cause it started bleeding. He asked me who Archie was. I told him he's met him and I had to say someone cause they were suspicious and looking at him. He asked again if I slept with his father and then he answered for me telling me of course I did. I held my nose as it throbbed until I was inside. I guess he felt guilty for hitting me cause he came and cleaned up my nose. He apologized for hitting me. Then he hugged me and rubbed my stomach. He told me he was coming back then he left. I rubbed the burn on my arm and I cried for my daddy. I sat on that chair for a long time crying and rubbing my arm. At one point I tried to stop and I couldn't stop crying. The baby started kicking me, probably because it was hungry, but I couldn't get it together. Eugene came in the door and I was in the dark in the same spot he left me in. I guess he felt sorry for me cause he put me in the bed and then he made something to eat and he made me eat. He told me that his parents messed around for a while and he doesn't know why they stopped. He said a little after he was born his mother met and married his stepfather. He hates his stepfather; he said daily he'd remind him that he wasn't his son. He said he and his stepbrother fought all the time. His stepfather mistreated him whenever his momma wasn't around. He asked about his father all of the time. His momma always said Malcolm didn't care. He said he had no idea that Whispers equaled Malcolm who he saw around all the time. He said one day he saw Whispers at the market when he was with his momma. He said it all came out, and he had to adjust to try to understand that Whispers was his father. He said he's got a lot of brothers and sisters but they're all in the city. He was the only one on this side of the Bay.

I told him everything I could think to tell him about my family. I was purging everything. Talking to him was the first time I allowed myself to admit how much I hated my momma. Immediately I felt guilty forever feeling like that about her but it was the truth. That night Eugene told me he loved me. I pretended like I didn't hear him, after all I just saw him with his arms around my sister. But my heart wouldn't stop beating. I was confused.

****

That was horrible! Why would my momma keep doing that knowing what was going to happen to her? The doctor held up my dark baby and said it was a boy. The second thing I noticed after his skin was his little thing. It was huge almost as big as him. Eugene is going to think the baby is his daddy's. If he started off this dark he was only going to get darker. His cry was angry like he was mad. He stared at me like he was trying to figure me out. Looking at him made me feel weird. I felt weak and vulnerable, I didn't like it. The nurse came in my room and she sat on my bed saying he was a beautiful baby. I looked at her like she was crazy. What would she know about colored babies to know which ones is beautiful and which ones wasn't. She cuddled him and snuggled with him as she smiled at him. I didn't understand it. I didn't get it.

****

Eugene came over one time looked at the baby. He looked at me, and then he walked out the door. That was a month ago. Then the landlord put a notice on the door saying my rent wasn't paid. I ran to my caseworker hysterical cause I couldn't go home. How could Eugene leave me with this baby when I didn't ask for this? I cried to my caseworker asking her to have somebody take the baby. She told me I didn't mean that and I just had the baby blues. She found a bed for the baby and I at a shelter. Archie came and took my furniture to his dad's garage temporarily until I could get into housing. How could Eugene get me pregnant on purpose and then run away when my baby came out the same color as his father? It's his fault my baby is BLACK! People look at the baby then they look at me. I'm brown Hershey chocolate brown. Most ask me why my baby so black. One girl thought it was funny to say I found an

African and had his baby. So I got on her about her cock eyed little girl. How come the main people who come talking trash can't take the dozens when they come back on them? She got in my face and it took three women to pull me off of her. I think my apartment came up first because they felt I was a danger to everyone else. Archie moved all my furniture in for me. He kept looking at the baby and smiling. He don't look at him like he's some black monster. The baby just stares at him and Archie gets a kick out of holding him. "Do you think he's mine?"

"Look at him, you almost light skinned."

"What difference that make? We all came from Africa. He could've reached way back in his roots and pulled out this warrior paint we call skin."

"Whatever, I don't know. I think he was conceived that day we were together, this skin makes me think he's not yours."

"If we got married he would be mine."

"Ugh! Archie let me think about it."

"What's to think about?"

"You want me to be something I'm not. You have no idea where I come from."

"Doesn't matter where you come from as long as you go with me."

"Right Archie, you're such a cornball."

Archie was excited enough for the both of us about the baby. The way he smiled at the baby is the way you would imagine a father looking at his child. My father never looked at any of us like that though. I sat there rubbing my burn asking myself why this scene made me mad.

Last Words

I inhaled then I blew smoke in the baby's face. The look he gives
me every time I do it makes me laugh. I know he wanna walk just
so he can smack it out of my hand. He squints his eyes just like his
daddy. I don't like when he does that. When I take him to the
doctors these nurses fall all over their selves trying to hold him.
 Don't matter if they white or colored they all love him. One of
them call herself being funny and asking me if I was American. I
cussed her out so badly; I wanted her to come around that desk so I
could show her what else came from Africa. The orderly was
holding me back while she sat there looking smug and like I was
ignorant and beneath her. When the orderly was walking me out he
told me I can't let people provoke me like that. He said she was
wrong and I could've filed a complaint with the hospital
administrator if I would've kept my cool. I told him the hospital
don't care how they treat us. He told me to wake up and pay
attention. He said times were changing and my baby could grow up
to be anyone. His eyes got big as he said my son could possibly be
President. Clearly this man is crazy. In a country that still treats us
like we're animals he wants to be ridiculous and waste time
dreaming. I didn't say anything else I just wanted to get away from
this clearly irrational idiot.

I met Jodi at the park with her baby. Jodi is the only one that I got
along with at the shelter. She got a little girl almost as dark as my
child. Her husband was in jail until a couple of weeks ago. She was
assigned an apartment in my building just in time for him to get
out. He seem kind of weak to me cause they always fussing. He
licks his lips at me whenever she's not looking. He's not even cute
and too weak for me to even consider him. "I need some money."

"For what?" We were pushing the babies in their swings.

"Food, my man be eating us out of house and home."

Eugene always made sure I had food when he was around. It would've hurt my feelings if he ate all my food and then left me hungry. "You should be thanking him. You finally losing weight."

She sucked her teeth, "I don't want to look like a little girl any more. I'm a woman, and I want to look like one."

"I don't look like a little girl."

"You ain't skinny neither." Then she exhaled, "look I need you to come to the store with me. I need you to push the stroller."

I raised an eyebrow, "push the stroller?"

"I'm gonna slip a few things in it as we go."

Jodi is the worst thief ever. I was mad when they put me in handcuffs as her accomplice. Jodi's man came and got their daughter but he wouldn't take my son. I had no one else to call so I called my momma's house. My momma answered and then she said she was on her way. She came with Jan who blurted out, "you did have Whispers' baby!" as soon as she saw him.

You could see dollar signs in my momma's eyes. "What did you name him?"

"Malcolm."

She frowned, "what kind of name is Malcolm?"

"I heard it and I liked it."

"You know where to go when you get out." Then I watched my momma and my sister walk out with my baby. My momma has gained a lot of weight. I guess she been eating more now that my father's gone.

I got out of county just in time to make it to my social worker's office for my monthly visit. I told her the baby had a cold so I left him with my momma.

When I got to my momma's house my brothers and nephews were all out on the porch. "Pam!" Fuzzy yelled as he came running towards me. I gave him a big hug. "I miss you."

"I got my own place you gonna have to come see me one of these days. Where's my baby?"

"Inside with Macio."

"Macio?" I frowned, "what he want with my baby?"

The closer we got to the house I could hear music playing. When I walked in the door, Malcolm was sitting in the middle of the floor watching Troy going to town punching Macio's hands. Macio was yelling and little Troy was going. Macio told him to hit harder. Melanie sat on the couch watching with sad eyes as her baby was sweating and moving faster than I've ever seen someone that little move. Belle was sitting next to Melanie with her arm around her son as they watch. "Switch!" Macio commanded. Troy stood next to his momma catching his little breath. Leonard walked over hands up like a boxer. When he hit Macio you heard it. Macio pulled his hand back and then he shook it. He had to tell Leonard to hold on cause he was coming for him.

"How old is he?" I asked Belle.

"He just turned five." She said proudly.

"And him?" I asked Melanie

"Three."

"Look at my little soldiers!" Macio said so proud. "Leo you trying to tear my hand off."

Leonard was waiting for Macio to tell him to go. My baby sat there watching like he was understanding what was going on. Macio told Leonard to go. Leonard direct fired rapidly on Macio. He was coming so fast and hard that he moved Macio backwards. Macio tried to hit Leonard and he knocked his hand out the way and hit him harder. Fuzzy came in the door smiling. Macio told Leonard to stop, Leonard wasn't breathing as hard as I thought he should've. Macio put gloves on Fuzzy and Leonard then he picked up Malcolm and he told him to watch as he told them to go. Fuzzy was bigger than little Leonard and he was hanging with him. Belle looked scared but proud of her son. When they were done Macio smiled at me. He told me he had to take my baby with him last night as he handled business. He held Malcolm like he was a proud father. Momma walked in the door, "when did you get out?"

"This morning."

"Explain to me how you end up in jail trying to get food for somebody else?"

"She's my friend." I said lowly.

"So much of a friend that she couldn't bail you out or take care of your son while you're in there behind her?" I looked at the floor. "You owe me money for watching him for you. How you gonna pay me back?"

"I don't have any money."

"Ask his father."

I exhaled, "what if he don't have it?"

"Then you'll have to work it off."

"I'll call him when I get home."

Then a car horn honked outside. Momma looked out the window. Tricey hurried out the door with a spaced out look on her face that I knew all too well. "Where's home?"

"I was in a shelter for a little bit."

"Macio, take them home. Don't come back until she tell you when she's gonna have my money." She gave him the keys to her car.

I asked Macio to take me to the market before we got home. He said he thought I didn't have money and I showed him my food stamps that I got this morning. While I was in the store Macio carried Malcolm showing him everything and explaining it to him like he understood him. I asked him why he keeps doing that. Macio told me to pay attention cause my son does. He said Malcolm watches everything and everybody. I told him that Malcolm does stare at me a lot but I didn't think that made him smart. Macio said the smart ones watch everything and everybody. Then I saw Eugene's friend watching us. He got in the checkout line behind us. When we got in the car Macio asked me who the guy was. I told him he was a friend of my ex. He asked me if I wanted him to handle the guy cause he was following us. I said no.

When we got to my place I called Archie. I asked him if he could help me out cause I owed money. Archie asked me how much I needed, and then he happily brought it over. I was so relieved; I didn't want my momma putting me on my back for nothing. I introduced Archie to my brother. Archie stayed with the baby while Macio took me back to momma. She snatched the money then she went back to her phone conversation. "That's not Malcolm's daddy." Macio smiled.

"How can you tell?"

"Jan says you were open for that man same color as Malcolm.

Personally I think Leonard and Malcolm got the same daddy."

"Why you think that?"

"They told me how he didn't want momma to get you while you was pregnant. Belle thinks so too even though he's blacker than night and little Leo is brown like her. They favor."

"All of you are crazy. Of course they favor they Momma's is sisters."

When I got back to my place Archie was pacing like he was late. I thought he was going to stay. He kissed my cheek and told me he'd see me later. I was a little disappointed that he didn't stay. I fed Malcolm then I put him to bed. The loud knock on my door scared me. My heart started pounding when I looked out the window and it was Eugene. I put the chain on the door and I cracked it. "What do you want?"

"I will break this door open if you don't open it." He growled.

"Go away Eugene!"

As I pushed the door closed he kicked it open. "You think I'm playing with you? This a game to you?"

Part of the doorframe hung from my door on the chain. "Are you crazy? You're going to fix that!"

"That's your fault I told you to open the door."

"What do you want?"

"Find a babysitter tomorrow, you're coming out with me."

"I can't fit none of my nice dresses."

He looked me over; "you are sweet thickness now aren't you?"

Then he looked around like something stunk. "What is that smell?" I didn't smell it. "Somebody smoke in here?"

"Me."

He looked mad, "I suggest you find another bad habit. I hate cigarettes."

"Besides you?"

He smiled, "yea. Besides me."

"Who says I care what you hate?"

"You miss me don't you?"

"You left me without anywhere to go. I was homeless and with the baby you gave me."

"That is not my baby." He pointed towards the back. "He too black. None of my other kids are black like that. What you name him anyways? I know you weren't stupid enough to try to name him Eugene."

"Malcolm," I watched his face.

"You're playing games! Why would you name him that?"

"Like you said I couldn't make him a junior. Besides everybody only knows your dad as Whispers."

His eyes danced around my body taking in my new form with appreciation. "You're still playing with fire."

I closed my door, "you can't come over here tearing up my place. How am I gonna fix this?" When he didn't respond I turned around and looked at him. He was staring at my body like he was lost in his thoughts. "Eugene! Did you hear me?"

"What?" He didn't hear a word I said.

"What's wrong with you?"

"I miss you!"

"Gross!" I missed him too but I was hurt more than I was anything else.

He frowned, "gross?"

"You give me a baby I didn't ask for and you broke up with me without even telling me. You let the landlord do your dirty work. Now you break my door and I'm supposed to care that you miss me? I'm not going nowhere with you. You don't pay for anything here, you can get out!"

He squinted his eyes at me. "You don't love me anymore?"

"You want me to tell you again what you did to me? Look at my door!"

"I'll fix your door."

"Try to talk to me when my door is fixed. Get out!"

"What?"

"You heard me!" Then I shoved him out the door.

I didn't sleep well all night. I was worried he wouldn't come back and I really wanted to see him. In the morning I got up early and showered. I didn't know for sure that Eugene was coming back, but I wanted to be ready just in case. I was bathing Malcolm in the sink. Macio was right he watches everything. He watched me walk in the room, he stared at my face when I picked him up and then he looked to see where I was taking him. He looked around the kitchen as I took his clothes and diaper off. He touched the water like he was aware of it. He watched me pick up the soap lather his rag and wash him. He kept watching my face. I wanted a cigarette so bad! I redirected my energy into getting ready just in case Eugene came over. I was getting ready to feed Malcolm when there was a loud knock on the door. I got excited when I saw that it was Eugene. I cracked the door then I sat down on the couch to feed the baby. Eugene had wood, nails, and stuff to fix my door. He looked at Malcolm eating for a minute not saying anything. Then he started working on the door. Whenever he turned around I pretended I was smiling at the baby. He does love me, or else he wouldn't have come back like I told him to. Malcolm sat quietly in my lap as we watched Eugene fix the door.

When he was done he walked over to us looking at the baby. He picked him up and held him out while he examined him closely. "All I see is Whispers. This is not my baby, sorry I tried."

"Eugene! How would that even be possible?"

"If you really want to go there we can otherwise you should leave it alone." He was still eyeing the baby.

I stood up. "No! You told me no men! No men! You were there! You know what you did! How can you say he's not yours? You have no right!"

Eugene kept looking from the baby to me. "Pam, it's not like it matters. I don't know how to be nobody's father. Belle is always mad at me behind her kid."

"But you don't deny hers, only mine." I felt empty. "I didn't ask to be nobody's momma. He's here and he deserves to know who his father is."

"Knowing my father hasn't changed my life all that much. I got my job on my own. I've been taking care of myself since I was young. The sooner this one realizes a black man is born without anyone to have his back the better off he'll be."

"A black man has a black woman to hold him down."

"All y'all do is bring complications. You whine, you complain, you make things impossible."

"My momma ain't no saint but she always had my daddy's back. Whatever he wanted she provided she always made sure he had what he needed. You just so quick to dismiss me, like you don't care."

"Cause I don't!"

"Then why are you here?"

He put the baby down on the floor and then he grabbed me by my face and kissed me. "Because you're good at what you do."

"That's the only reason?"

"I told you this ain't no love connection." My feelings were so hurt. He tried to kiss me again and I backed away from him. "Pam! Don't act all sensitive! I've always been honest with you."

"I had your baby! You knew my father died and you didn't even tell me. You kept me locked up in that apartment for what?"

"I didn't ask you to have my baby. Your father didn't care about you, and you know your momma don't care. You the stupid one going over there and almost getting your butt kicked for nothing. Don't nobody over there even like you. Belle told me how you always lie and steal."

"My daddy loved me!"

"Then why he let your momma put you out there? Turning tricks before you even understand what sex is. I see how you could confuse this for love, you ain't ever had it. But I don't love you. I love what you do."

I started crying, "get out!"

He looked surprised by my reaction. "What?"

"Get out!"

"If I leave I'm not coming back!"

"Good! How dare you get me pregnant on purpose and then treat me like this. My momma and my daddy love me! Belle just mad cause I'm prettier than her. She's always been jealous of me. You don't know half the things there are to know about her. You so quick to say you know her baby is yours when you should be questioning her not me. You may have broke her in, but you weren't the only one!" I was lying but he hurt me, so it's my job to hurt him just as badly.

Eugene looked angry and he was silent for a minute. I moved to pick up the baby who was silently watching us. Eugene grabbed me by my neck and threw me as hard as he could into the couch, my head hit the wall. "You are nothing but a liar! Stop trying to hurt me!"

"You're trying to hurt me!" I held on to my head. "You don't want him. What makes you think I do? I didn't want no babies!"

"Then you should've kept your legs closed!" I looked at him. "Who you gonna get to keep him?"

"For what?"

"You're going out with me tonight. We can spend the night at my place. I'll bring you home in the morning." I didn't respond. He reached in his pocket and pulled out money. "Advance payment for tonight." He put the money on the coffee table. "Go get a dress." Then he left.

The baby crawled over to me watching my face like he felt bad for me. He pulled up on my gown and stood there looking at me looking like his daddy. I got irritated and kicked him, I bet if the baby wasn't so black he'd treat me better.

I called Macio and asked him if the baby could hang out with him over night. I could hear his smile over the phone. Macio actually liked my baby, which was weird cause he didn't like any of the others outside of training them. I told him he could spend the night at my place cause I wasn't coming home until the morning.

Eugene loved my new dress and he cut our night short to take me back to his house. We had sex all over his house. When he dropped me off in the morning he gave me more money telling me I earned every dollar. His comment made me feel worse. He told me he loved me even if he tried to act like he never said it. Macio, the baby, and some girl were sleep in my bed when I came home. I was too tired to care. I laid on the couch and went to sleep.

****

"Who's up next?" The tall light skinned man asked.

I stood up and little Malcolm followed me. "We are. I just need you to cut it all off." Malcolm's hair had gotten bigger than his face. I was combing it, but Macio said he looked homeless. He told me to come here to get Malcolm's haircut. Macio was going on and on about how chocolate men couldn't walk around looking raggedy. I didn't really care, but Macio was going to get mad if he repeated himself.

"Alright," he looked down at Malcolm. "He's a little thing, he gonna sit still? I don't have time to be fighting with no babies!" He huffed.

I looked at Malcolm who was taking everything in. "He'll be fine I promise."

The guy put a big box and a phone book in the seat to make Malcolm just tall enough to sit in his chair. I put Malcolm in the seat and I told him not to move. Malcolm watched in the mirror as the guy put the drape on him. "What's your name?" The guy asked.

"Malcolm."

"Well Malcolm today must be your lucky day. You are getting your first professional haircut by the BEST barber in all of Oakland!" Malcolm watched him in the mirror while the guy picked out his hair. "When you get your hair cut you have to come to the best. You need to tell your momma to bring you to Moses only." Then he looked me up and down. "You gonna be the one bringing him or is your husband gonna come sometimes?" I blank stared at him. "Aw! Don't look at me like that. You too pretty not to be smiling." The other guys in the shop were paying close attention to our conversation. I didn't like being on display like this. "How about this," he smiled at me. "I'll cut his hair for free this time if you give me one smile." My face didn't change. "Oh come on sweet thang. Give us a little smile." I forced a smile. "There now that wasn't so hard was it?" Malcolm turned to watch each instrument he picked up and then what he did with it. "You's a nosey little somebody ain't you." He said to Malcolm. Malcolm watched him without a smile. "Tada!" He turned Malcolm towards me.

"How much?"

"I told you, that smile paid the bill. Make sure you bring your little man back to Moses when you come."

I said thank you then I took Malcolm back to my momma's house to show Macio his fresh haircut. Macio went on and on telling Malcolm he looked good. He told him his lines were straight and then he showed Malcolm in the mirror what he was talking about. I rolled my eyes cause it's a waste of breath to explain all that to a baby. Macio always talking to him like Malcolm could ever know what he was talking about. Momma asked who cut Malcolm's hair. Macio told her that he told me to go to Cuts on McArthur. Momma looked at me then she asked how much I paid for the cut. So I told her what happened. "Moses is tall and light skinned?"

"Yes."

"He liked you?" She smiled.

"I guess."

"You like him?"

I exhaled; I already knew what she was thinking. "Momma please!"

She frowned at me, "please what? He's got connections."

"Oh yea? Like what?" Macio asked.

"He can connect you to a herb man."

"Herb?"

"Grass, weed, Herb." She said like she was talking to Malcolm. "You need it, he got it. And it sounds like he likes your sister."

"Pam you gonna get your brother the hook up?"

"Man momma! Why it always gotta be me?" I fussed.

Momma slapped me hard then she waited for me to straighten up. "After all your brother does for you, why wouldn't you do this for him?"

"You know it's hard for me to sleep." Macio chimed in.

"Besides you know you like laying with people. I don't know why you try to act like you don't."

"I don't like being pimped out by my own momma."

"Oh whatever! You'd rather be stupid like Belle? You know that guy hasn't come for her in seems like forever. The good girl act gets old."

"You gonna get me the hook up or not? I mean I take care of your boy like a father and everything."

"Can you stop screwing females in front of him? He was humping on my friend's little girl the other day."

Macio smiled, "Cat Daddy! Give me some skin!" He said to Malcolm. "He's a Latour, I'm showing him how to handle his gift."

"He don't need to be worried about girls, he's not even in school yet. You gonna have him running around like the happy humper. Jumping on all the girl's legs."

"Ok, ok. Are you gonna get me the hook up or not?"

"You gonna protect me if this big ole guy starts acting crazy?"

"Of course." He smiled.

Two weeks later I took Malcolm for another haircut. Moses couldn't take his eyes off of me from the time I walked in the door. This time I was all smiles and Moses wanted to do anything I asked. All those guys in there were looking with big eyes and telling Moses he was a lucky son of a gun. I told him I couldn't stop thinking about him since the last time I met him. He kept inhaling and exhaling like he was proud. "You married?"

"Yes, but she knows what I do. When can I take you out?"

I smiled to myself; since he's married he wouldn't be bothering me at all hours of the night or whatever. "When you wanna go?"

"I could pick you up after I get off over here."

I put my hand on my hip. "And where do you think you're supposed to be taking me?"

He smiled, "we could get a drink. I know a spot. I just wanna be your friend."

I agreed then I wrote down my address. Macio came over to hang out with Malcolm while I was gone. Macio opened the door and introduced himself. I could tell Moses was trying to size him up. Macio was my only short brother, and he's the craziest. People underestimate his size all the time. That's how he ended up killing someone on the base and getting his dishonorable discharge after serving a little time. They said he wasn't mentally stable, but momma says Macio is fine.

Moses took me to a bar where he spent most of the time talking about himself. How fine he is, how his kids look like him, how he's the best barber ever. When I yawned he asked me why I was tired it wasn't even six yet. I told him I've been having trouble sleeping, etc. He went over to the pay phone then he came back all proud. A little while later another guy came in the bar. Moses introduced me to Casper. Casper asked Moses what he needed. Moses told him I only needed grass. He asked which one as he rattled off names. Moses smiled at me and told him to give me a specific one. Casper smiled and said he'd be back. Moses told me to let him know when I needed more and he'd be happy to make sure I had what I needed. His friend came back and then he slipped something into my purse. Moses almost lost his mind when I pressed up against him and hugged him thanking him for his help. That was all I had to do, and I was happy. I didn't feel like doing anything with him, and he was going to have to do more than give me some grass if he wanted some of my sweet stuff.

I watched Macio break it down and then roll it up. He said Moses got me the good stuff. Then he took a few puffs and he looked like he felt so good. I asked him to let me have some. He said it wasn't for girls and I was gonna end up like Tricey all strung out. I told him grass wasn't gonna do that to me. After so many days of begging Macio finally gave me some to shut me up. I remember choking and looking at Malcolm when the sweetest sensation came over me. All the heartache from missing Eugene lifted. The disappointment from seeing Archie with that girl lifted too. Looking at Malcolm didn't irritate me in this space. Everything felt good and Macio and I had the deepest conversation ever. He told me stuff about my parents I didn't know. Like the first time he saw our father kill someone. When momma was just daddy's sweet thing on the side to when she became his everything. Momma would make stuff happen for our father where his wife at the time was just pretty. Macio said seeing all the stuff going on he didn't want no pretty woman. I told him I always wondered why he was with ugly girls. He said we be having all these guys open just because we're pretty. He don't want those problems. He said his ugly girls be so happy to have him in their lives that they do whatever he say. He say he ain't gotta marry nobody and he refuses to get married. I never thought about getting married, but if I was going to marry I'd want to marry Eugene. Malcolm sat quietly on the couch watching us like he was taking everything in. Macio thanked me for giving him Malcolm and I frowned at him. He said he can't make babies, and from the moment he saw Malcolm who's only a few shades darker than him he's felt like he was his. He said the other boys were too much of Momma's boys.

When I woke up Malcolm was all snuggled up into me. His little black body looked all peaceful. I never let him sleep with me or ever get this close to me. It makes me feel weak whenever I tried to hug him or something. Normally I just want him away from me.

****

"Where did you get all this furniture?" Melanie asked.

"My ex," I watched her look around my place. "It's going to be interesting being neighbors."

"Yeah, but it will be good for the boys." She said sadly. "Momma says you're going to bring me problems. Can we make a deal? I'll keep Malcolm for you as much as you need or want. Please don't cause me problems."

"Did we grow up in the same house? Why are you so weak?"

"We are different people."

"Whatever, it would be great to have a backup when Macio can't watch him."

"Momma, can me and Malcolm go play?"

"Troy if I open this door and I can't see you I'm gonna beat your little butt."

"Yes momma. Come on Malcolm." Troy said.

Malcolm looked at us and then he followed Troy. "Can Malcolm talk?"

I blew air, "of course he can. I've even heard him speaking Spanish when he plays with those Mexican kids. I don't think he knows what he's saying though probably just mimicking the sounds."

"I've never heard him say anything."

"Guess he hasn't needed to say anything to you. He watches people more than he speaks though. He gets on my nerves. It's like he's judging me."

"That's your baby, your child loves you. He's too young to judge you."

The door was still open slightly and then Belle walked in. She rolled her eyes at me then she smiled at Melanie. "Thank you Melanie, Leonard is out there with the boys." She started backing up.

"Wait! When are you coming back?"

"Boomer is taking me to Los Angeles to meet his momma. I don't know how long we'll be gone."

"Where are his clothes for school?"

"Don't you have clothes for him?"

"Yeah packed in a box somewhere."

"Have her help you." She gestured towards me. "I gotta go Boomer is waiting."

"Does Eugene know you replaced him with Boomer?"

Belle's eyes turned evil, "if I saw Eugene I would tell him. Maybe you can tell him the next time you go out tricking."

"At least I get paid for what I do. You out there giving it away for free. And now you have that low life's baby."

Shock and surprise spread across Belle's face. "How do you know?"

"Your face is all fat! Ray Charles can see that you pregnant. You always try to act like you're better than me just because momma didn't put you out. The only difference between you and me is that I actually know what to do and I get paid very well for it. What's between your legs ain't no different than what any other female got. Your technique is the only thing that will make you stand out. I don't know how you thought having a baby was going to keep a man like Eugene around."

She was angry and stepped closer. "Is Malcolm Eugene's son?"

"You the one with the golden cooch! I could never be good enough for Eugene." She took another step. "Take one more step in my direction and I won't care that you're pregnant!"

Belle knew I wasn't lying. Her eyes watered and then she started crying. Melanie and I looked surprised. "I hate you Pam! You always go out of your way to hurt me. I hate you! You're my sister!" Then she hurried out the door leaving it open.

Melanie's eyes were still big then she looked out the door. She asked me who the little girls were. There were two little girls playing with our boys. I told her they lived here. Then I asked her why Belle cried. She reminded me of what it's like when you're pregnant, you cry a lot. Then Melanie looked at me with tearful eyes. I backed away from her. Then she thanked me for being the only person to help her when she was pregnant. When she told me she loved me it made me feel weird. I spoke fast and then I left. One of the little girls kept putting her arms around Malcolm I guess cause he was the littlest one. He kept wiggling out her arms and trying to get away from her. That made her chase him. I never would've played with somebody that black I don't know what her problem was.

I was smoking a cigarette in front of the door watching these fast little girls chase our boys and kiss on them. Macio came stomping into the courtyard. He looked angry as he walked up on me. I put my cigarette out and braced myself. Momma could've lied on me again who knows why he's mad. Macio walked in my face and asked why I didn't bring Malcolm for training this morning. I told him I couldn't get out the bed this morning. Jodi came over with drinks last night and this morning I was sick. Macio got in my face and he told me to call him next time. I asked him why he was so mad. He called Malcolm over interrupting his game of chase with the little girl. When Troy and Leonard saw Macio they came over as well. Macio told Malcolm to punch me. Malcolm hesitated and then he looked at Macio. Leonard asked Macio why he would tell Malcolm to hit his momma? Macio told him I wasn't nobody and I was interfering with his training. Malcolm squinted at Macio and said no. Macio flinched at the boys and none of them jumped. Macio pulled off his belt and started swinging. Malcolm didn't run from him but he looked mad. I couldn't tell if he was madder at Macio for hitting him or me for not protecting him. When he motioned towards Troy, Troy ran across the yard super fast to his momma's apartment. Leonard stepped in and told Macio to back up. Leonard got beat too. Leonard and Malcolm stood there looking at Macio with the same evil squint. Macio hit me a couple times telling me I was lazy and worthless. I went inside my apartment cause I didn't need my neighbors seeing me get beat on by my brother. When I heard Melanie outside going off like a protective mother would, I peeked out the window. Melanie had something in her hands that she was threatening to hit Macio with. She was yelling telling him she never gave him permission to hit her son. Macio took a step in Melanie's direction and Troy lost it. Seeing Troy react Leonard and Malcolm sided with Troy. They knocked Macio down and then they hit him a few times then Melanie told all the boys to run with her to her apartment. Why didn't they try to protect me? Macio got up going off! I took a deep breath then I opened the door. Macio was barking at me and any neighbors who weren't outside before we're now watching. I kept asking Macio to calm down but he wouldn't. He didn't see which way Melanie ran and he didn't know which apartment was hers so he told me to tell him which one. I was scared cause he looked crazy, but I didn't say. He beat on me until someone made him stop. As he left he told me to make sure Malcolm was at training. Melanie ran out and immediately thanked me for protecting them. She helped me inside then she cleaned me up. Jodi came down to check on me. She offered me grass to help me deal with my swollen face and the pain. Melanie shook her head no at me, but I was hurting and I needed to deal with what just happened here. Melanie told Malcolm to come with her. He stood there staring at me for a minute. I don't know why he does that. It's like he's dissecting everything about me when he does that. He watched me take a hit. This stuff was stronger, I asked Jodi what was in it and she said her man said it was a cocktail. Melanie called Malcolm to come one more time. When I was totally relaxed he hugged me then he followed Melanie out.

Chapter 5

"Can I have some more?" I tilted my glass.

The unfriendly guy hesitated then he poured more. "Drink more, talk less."

I laughed, which quickly turned into a cry. "I got some stuff to get off my chest! I gotta tell somebody and you're the only person here." He blank stared at me. "Why he send you? You too pretty to get your hands dirty like this." I looked at his wedding band. "You probably got a family too. How could you do this?"

"My momma hugged me. My momma's never been against me."

"I ain't never been against my son."

"He's your son now that he's the only one who could save you. You just said how you abused him and wouldn't give him the decency of a hug." He ran his hand over his face. "Just stop talking, let the pills do their job."

"My talking bothers you? I bet as long as I don't run I can sit here running my mouth until I pass out and there's nothing you could do about it!" He didn't respond, he kept looking at me. "What do I wanna tell you next? Oh, ok... So..."

~

"Man! Moses you are the MAN!" The guy said giving Moses a high five. "Your lady is *dynamite*!" He drooled at me.

These guys looked hungry and Moses has to be an idiot if he trust them. I just wanted to get my stuff and go. Moses wasn't getting *none* tonight, I was not in the mood for the let down. "Thank you! Thank you!" Moses said like he could take credit for my beauty. "Check this out, she got a son. He's a little fella, but he's good. I was thinking you could put him on the team."

"What team?" Moses gets on my nerves. He's always planning stuff for me like he thinks I'm just going to go along with whatever he says. I've went off on him so many times for doing this it's not even funny.

"Football." The second guy said. "You haven't heard of the Richmond Steelers? We're number three in our division."

"Richmond? NO! Why should I care about Richmond when I live in Oakland?"

"Aw foxy lady, it's all good! Don't be like that." The first guy said.

"We'll teach him discipline and how to be a team player."

"My son already knows all of that."

"From who? You? What you know about teaching a man to be a man? We're trying to offer you help with your son. Moses says his daddy ain't around much. We come in to help."

I curled my lips, "Moses don't speak for me. My son is fine and don't need no suspicious looking guys talking about you can help him. My son don't play games!"

"Relax baby! We wasn't trying to ruffle your feathers. We were just trying to pitch in and help our community where we see a need." He patted my hand, "how about we do this. Next time Moses, bring them out to checkout our practice. Let her see how organized we are and then she can make an informed decision."

"Why you talking like that? Slithering in your words." These guys were not on the up and up. The fact that they thought they could talk down to me annoyed me.

I let Moses convince me to bring Malcolm. Troy begged me to bring him too. Melanie didn't trust Moses so she insisted that she had to come as well. When we got to the practice the boys on the field were running in place and taking orders. When the guys told them to drop, they dropped. If they said run, they ran. Malcolm and Troy looked unimpressed as they watched the twenty plus kids run around the field. "Moses! You brought two? He shoots, and he scores."

Melanie and I looked at Moses to let him put them straight, but he smiled and accepted their praise. Troy looked angry, but Malcolm told him to be cool. "Hey little man, you two wanna see if you can hang with the big kids?"

"No thanks." Troy said crossing his arms.

The first guy's face twitched like he was trying to hold his temper back. "No thanks?" He gestured to the field. "These are the Richmond Steelers, number three in their division. Next season we will be number one. The fact that we invited you at all should twist your cap back cat."

Melanie pointed at the boys on the field, "what does punching and kicking have to do with football?"

His eyes turned evil, "that's what's wrong with you. Why are you questioning a man?"

"You can't talk to my momma like that, I don't care who you supposed to be." Troy stood up ready to go. Malcolm stood next to him.

"Calm down Craig he just a little nigga. It ain't worth breaking him down." The other guy said as he tried to stare at Malcolm and Troy who would not back down.

"Craig, Moose, I don't know what got into these kids, but they ain't what you looking for." Moses said standing up.

"Don't let me catch you on the street little nigga! I'll break you down and then have you crawling back to your momma!" Craig said.

"OR! We could handle this right here and now! Don't nobody talk to my momma like they crazy!" Troy said.

"Troy! Come on! I don't want y'all fighting your way out of here. You can't win this. Those two are killers, you'll get your hat twisted back so fast." Moses said.

"Sounds to me like y'all don't know who the Latour's are! Before you ever think you can you need to ask somebody who we are." Troy said sounding like a man. Even I looked at him like *WELL*!

The guys walked away looking completely pissed off. We started walking towards Moses' car. I knew those guys weren't going to just let us go. Two teenage looking boys who were sitting in the bleachers watching the whole scene came out. They didn't say nothing, they just came. Troy told his momma to get in the car, and then he and Malcolm started fighting these boys two times they size each. They broke them down, face down on the ground and then they got in the car. I told Moses to drive as Moose and Craig came running.

Moses was going off talking about they were business acquaintances and that Malcolm and Troy showed no respect. Melanie was quiet for a long time, and then she had enough. "SHUT UP MOSES! You would've let that guy hit me for asking him an obvious question. You truly are yellow!"

Now why she say that? Moses started swerving and then he tried to reach back towards Melanie. Troy wasn't having that. Moses pulled over on San Pablo Avenue the main busy street that connects all the way from Oakland through Richmond. He kicked us out of his car going off as he sped away. Troy called Macio from the payphone. I told them not to tell Macio that Moses was mad at me. Cause it was going to be problems if Macio thought he wasn't going to get his weed like he's supposed to. I made up some stupid lie about getting on the wrong bus and being stranded. Macio looked at me out the corner of his eyes and then he turned up the radio. He sang a long, "someone picked you from the bunch one glance was all it took. Now it's much too late for me to take a second look." He sang the song like it was talking for him. He asked Melanie if he could use her phone, then he left happily singing the song.

In the morning Melanie asked if Malcolm could help her go grocery shopping. Malcolm was hurrying out the door and I hadn't said yes. I laid back down and peacefully fell asleep. Then someone banged on the door. The pounding jarred me out of my sleep. I ran to the door and it was Eugene and he looked pissed. I didn't even invite him in and he just walked in. "You hanging out with Mason's now?"

"Who?"

"Tell me about your little trip to Richmond yesterday." He was mad.

"How do you even know about that?"

"Never mind that! Answer me!"

"It's not none of your business who I hang with."

Eugene squinted at me then he grabbed me and threw me on the couch. My robe flew open and his eyes scanned me. "Craig and the rest of his family ain't no good. They use that football team as a cover for the runners they recruit. They a bunch of hot heads running them Richmond streets. You need to stay out of there!"

"What difference does it make? It's not like you care!"

"Don't make me hurt you Pam! Stay away from them and stay out of Richmond. The Mason's and the Baker's run Richmond. You don't understand the game out there. Stay out of there."

"Admit that you care first," I smiled at him.

Eugene almost gasped at my comment. He wasn't expecting me to say that. On that note he turned on his heels and walked away. I shut my door and chuckled all the way back to my bed.

Moses snuck over in the evening with treats for me and Macio as he apologized for letting his temper get the best of him.

****

I tried to grab my composure, I didn't want to be here but the principal said they called my momma when they couldn't reach me at first. I concentrated on my steps so I wouldn't stagger when the receptionist stood to show me into the principal's office. She has that look of shame on her face, but I wasn't planning on being here. Shoot! They should know parents have lives! When I walked in the door my momma, Belinda, and Melanie were sitting in front of the principal's desk. The secretary brought a chair in for me. "Thank you Ms. Latour. Now we can begin." She looked at all of us one by one. "Ms. Latour," she was looking at Belle. "Your son has always been a pleasure. He's very smart, but he has one mean temper. We've spoken about it before. Mrs. Davis son is so sweet, he struggles in school but he's normally a good kid." Then she looked at me. "Ms. Latour I've told you that everyone here thinks your son is brilliant. Sometimes he hangs out in our library for fun. He's a speed reader and he has such a thirst for knowledge, I'd hate to see all of that go down the drain behind incidents like this." Then she exhaled. "Your son is very sensitive to comments made about his complexion. He viciously attacked a student today for simply making a comment about it."

I started laughing, I was trying to hold it back but I couldn't. "I bet you no one else will be that dumb."

The Principal looked irritated. "Ms. Latour this is serious! That kid had to be rushed to the hospital."

"Your point? You've seen Malcolm, he's black. No he's blacker than black. That kid should've kept his mouth shut."

"The way he hurt that child was not ok."

"Listen! I don't care! Malcolm knows how ugly his skin is. I remind him everyday. Ain't nobody gonna love him walking around looking like that, but I bet you they gonna respect him." The principal sat there looking mad. I laughed again, "Oh you mad now?"

"I happen to think your son is beautiful and exactly the way God created him."

"God? God ain't had nothing to do with the creation of that one. Shoot! He turned his back on our whole family of savages."

"Pam!" My momma said, "please excuse my daughter. Had I known she was high I never would've let her come down here."

"You the reason I'm high! Like you care. As long as I keep money in your pockets you don't care."

My momma gave me a death stare. "If her son was the one fighting why are we here?" Belle asked.

"The fight escalated and both of your boys were involved as well. It's thought that some of your other grandchildren were here, but I can't prove that. I need to be able to assure parents that this school environment is a safe place for them to bring their children to.

Leonard will be going to middle school soon enough, but I need to know that the rest of you will get control over your children."

"This school will be safe when you punish kids for teasing others. Telling them sticks and stone may break your bones but words will never hurt you is a load of **crap**! **Words hurt**! **They hurt**! **They stay in your brain, and they jump out at you when you least expect it**. **Words *haunt* you**! They beat you down! They cripple you!"

The principal stared angrily at me. "This is coming from the woman who just said she's the main person telling her son he's ugly! You are the problem here. That poor boy deserves to be loved, and clearly he doesn't get that from you!"

"You don't know what he gets from me." I got mad, "do your job and protect these dumb kids who don't know who to mess with and who to leave alone." She kept staring at me. "Keep looking at me I'ma come around this desk and fix your face for you. My son gets it from somewhere."

"Pam," momma pretended like she didn't like what I said. "So you think my grandson is brilliant?" I could see the stars in my momma's eyes.

"Momma Shuga, yes." She opened Malcolm's student file. "Look at all of his markings, and his teacher's comments. He's a real good boy too. He doesn't distract the class and he's normally very quiet." She smiled, "when he talks about his assignments he comes to life though. His teacher gives him special assignments. Mr. Smith says he enjoys creating challenges for Malcolm. Your grandson can be anyone he wants to be. But he's going to have to work on his tolerance of other people. Some people are going to be down right rude." She looked at me, "some people don't understand how truly beautiful black can be."

I started to go after this woman and my momma grabbed me. "Well now, we got a little bit of all shades in our family. We got a few light skins and then you know Malcolm. I think we got the rainbow of brown covered." She told me to sit down. "I think the point that my daughter is failing to make is that we will control our boys, but you need to control your students. Malcolm knows what he looks like, and he don't need nobody pointing it out to him. Hopefully the whole school has learned that Malcolm has no patience for teasing. Like you said, he's smart and he comes here to learn. If they leave him alone, he will leave them alone."

When we walked out of the office we went to the library. My nieces and nephews were quietly talking while Malcolm sat over in the corner reading a book. I picked up the book thinking it might've been at least a little interesting and it was some kind of history book. I slammed the book on the table. He looked mad that I took his book but he didn't say anything. I made Malcolm walk with me in the other direction cause I didn't want to hear whatever my momma had to say. Malcolm kept looking at me while we walked. He didn't say anything he just looked at me. As we approached a deli next to the drug store I remembered I needed some more condoms for when I saw Moses tomorrow. As we approached the drug store, "it's Fuzzy." He pointed to Fuzzy who was sweeping the front of the deli with an apron on.

"Fuzzy? You got a job?" I smiled.

"Yep, nobody in that house cares whether I eat or not. I gotta do what I gotta do."

"How you like it?"

"It's not bad."

Then a white girl walked out with shoulder length brown hair. "Can you help me move boxes?" She stopped talking when she saw Malcolm. "You are **BEAUTIFUL**!" She exclaimed.

Malcolm and I held the same WHATEVER expression as we looked at her. "I can help you." Malcolm volunteered.

"Are you looking for a job?" She finally looked at me. "Hello I'm Rita."

"Pam."

"Yes." Malcolm said.

"Are you his mother? Is it ok with you if he works for us?"

"What you going to hire this little boy to do?"

"Oh we have plenty of jobs for him to do. We need dishes washed, tables bussed, all kinds of things. We'd love to have him if it's ok with you?"

"Of course, how soon can he start?" I was happy to get rid of him.

"Today if he wants. Let me go tell my father." She quickly walked back inside.

"You better not embarrass me in front of these white people!" I said through clinched lips.

Malcolm stared at me; Fuzzy put his arm around Malcolm. "I'll look out for him, but these are nice people." Then Fuzzy smiled bigger, "maybe Troy and Leonard will want to work here too."

"So what they gonna do, hire all the Latour's?"

"They could."

"Whatever, Fuzzy will you walk him home?"

"Sure, I'll make sure he's ok." Then he looked at Malcolm and smiled, "you know how to sweep?" Malcolm looked at him like he had to be joking.

Rita's father came out and thanked me for letting my son work for them. He said they needed the help badly. He told me how much he planned to pay Malcolm and that he would pay him every Friday. He said they needed more help so if we knew of anyone trustworthy to send them his way.

When I went into the drugs store I was standing in front of the condoms trying to steady myself cause my high was still going. Then she walked by, she looked like African royalty. Her skin was a pretty dark chocolate brown. Her hair was pulled back into a low bun, and her clothes were real fine. The way she talked to the pharmacist was like she wasn't nervous about talking to white people. Her tone was proper, but kind of country proper. My mouth watered when I noticed her big ring on her finger. She was probably married to some uppity black guy. I wanted her ring, and I stood there asking myself how much of a pushover did I think she was. I thought about snatching her ring and running, but I was in no condition to do that. I would just walk up on her hit her and as she cowered I'd take her ring and walk away. I started imagining how important, special, loved, and good I'd feel with that ring on my finger. When the lady turned around she was smiling with her prescription in her hand. When her eyes met mine her smile dropped. She stood there for a minute taking me in. Then the look that her eyes gave me was like she was telling me she wished I was that stupid. She stood there for a minute looking at me like she could take me. I smiled at her cause I was in no shape to fight right now, and then I turned my back. I looked out the window and she got in a very fancy car, then she waved at the Rita girl and her father as she drove off.

****

I was talking to Melanie and Jodi in the courtyard. Melanie finally

97

heard from Troy's father. She was upset cause all he wanted to talk about was hooking up; he had no interest in meeting his son. Melanie was cursing him when we heard the boys coming. Malcolm had a bag in his hands and they were all excited. "What are you little devils up to?" Jodi asked.

"Hi momma." Troy said coming and giving his momma a kiss on the cheek.

"Hi baby, what's in the bag?"

"Malcolm's gonna cut my hair."

"What?" I laughed, "Malcolm don't know how to cut hair. You might as well wait for Moses to get here in a little bit."

All the boys smiled, "is he bringing his cousin?" Leonard smiled.

"And that's why you can't come over while she's here. Nasty little boy." I frowned.

Leonard smiled as he snapped his fingers while the rest of the boys held sneaky grins. Troy got a chair and sat it in the middle of the grass. Malcolm put batteries in the Clippers he bought. "What if he messes up?" Melanie was nervous.

"Then we'll cut it off." Then Troy looked at Malcolm. "Don't mess up!"

Malcolm combed out Troy's hair like Moses does. When Malcolm turned on the clippers Troy grabbed his hand as he yelled, "Wait!" He took fast scared exaggerated breaths. He told Malcolm he was trusting him not to make him look crazy. Malcolm told him to relax. Troy screamed when the clippers touched his hair. He said the sound was making him crazy. Malcolm was focused and holding his arms just like he observed Moses doing. Fuzzy started laughing halfway through which cause Troy to shoot out of the seat. He was panicking asking if Malcolm nicked him. All the boys laughed, even Malcolm laughed. I told Troy Fuzzy was messing with him and his hair looked good. Malcolm looked at me for a minute. I guess I don't compliment him normally. Troy sat down and Malcolm finished cutting. Moses and his little cousin came, as Malcolm was about to line Troy up. He told Malcolm to hold on then he gave him a little instruction. Malcolm didn't say anything but you could tell he wasn't getting new information. Malcolm lined Troy up then Leonard held the mirror in front of Troy as he told Malcolm he was next. Troy asked Melanie if she liked his hair. She told him she loved it and he looked very handsome. Moses was too busy trying to critique Malcolm than being ready to go. Fuzzy was talking in a low voice trying to talk in Carole's ear. She was all smiles and I shook my head at them. Moses didn't want to leave until Malcolm was done. He seemed a little jealous that Malcolm picked up naturally what he's worked to master. Fuzzy and Leonard left and Troy went home with his momma. Carole asked Malcolm what he wanted to eat as we walked out the door. Moses stayed huffy all night. We went to his bar, had some drinks, and then he took me out to dinner. I don't mind going out with Moses and working him for everything I could get. As long as I made him feel he was the best he was open to anything even if I don't feel like putting out. He still comes running as long as I stroke his ego. Sex with Moses was not even good, no adventure or anything. He always has to be on top and when he drinks it's over as soon as it begins.

Moses sat up and asked me who was walking up on us. I turned to see Eugene my heart fluttered. "Who's this?"

"This is my friend Moses. Moses this is Malcolm's father."

Eugene frowned at me, "let you tell it. Why you stop calling me?"

"You're never home, and then a female answered the last time. Why would I keep calling?"

"Now she's here with me so she has no reason to call you." Moses interjected.

"Shut up before I gut you like a fish!" Then Eugene looked at me. "Call me again."

Moses stood up tall and husky. "Maybe you don't recognize me, but I'm not to be messed with."

"I don't care who you are," men stood up at the table Eugene came from. "Sit down!"

Moses turned red but he kept standing. Our waiter came, Moses put money in his hand to cover the bill then he told me we were leaving. I looked at Eugene and he was smirking at Moses. When I stood up Eugene told me to call him. Moses was mad and grumbling all the way back to my place. I told Moses to sit on the couch and then I went to Malcolm's room. The door was open and Malcolm had that little girl's legs spread as he worked her. I opened my mouth but no sound came out. Malcolm's just a little boy and this girl's a teenager older than Fuzzy. Moses was mad sitting on the couch; I walked in the room and shut the door behind me. Malcolm looked at me but it was like he didn't care. I told him to stop that and her uncle was in the other room. He said so, as he kept going. I popped him upside the head and told him to get off of her. Carole got up fast and I told her to fix her hair and her clothes. I told her she needed to be ashamed of herself and she dropped her head while she smiled at Malcolm. Malcolm was sitting there naked and ok his body didn't look like a eight year old's body but he is. I told Malcolm to open the window and then he needed to get in the bed. I looked at Carole and I told her if she didn't want me to tell on her she needed to be cool. Carole was a pretty little girl; I didn't understand why this teenager was having sex with a little boy. I thought maybe Fuzzy or heck even Leonard they're closer to her age. "A little boy Carole?"

She smirked, "*sorry*?" She shrugged.

I wanted to beat her, but then Moses would know. And it wouldn't matter why all momma would know is Macio's not getting his weed and she'd come after me. I swatted her as hard as I could on her butt. Yea! Now that smirk was gone and her eyes got big. She took a deep breath and said bye to Malcolm as she opened the door as if everything was ok. That's when I realized this has been going on for a while, that's the same tone she always had when we came back. Moses asked what they were doing and she told him she was telling Malcolm a bedtime story. Moses didn't even question her. He looked at me then he told me not to call Eugene. I gave him a yeah-right look. "He don't do nothing for Malcolm anyways why would you call him?"

"You don't know what he does and what he doesn't." Moses started huffing, "look Moses I like you. You're good to me and we have fun. But as long as you're walking out that door to go home to your wife you can't tell me what to do with my time when you're not around. Especially when it comes to him."

Moses turned fire engine red, then he grabbed me by my neck. I punched him in the face and started kicking. Carole started screaming and then Malcolm came flying out the room with a steel bat. He hit big ole Moses and he dropped. Malcolm hit Moses one more time and you heard it. Moses put his hands up in surrender. Malcolm told him to get out! Moses looked at Malcolm like he was trying to understand where all that power came from. I was surprised he came out with anything after all the stuff I see Macio make them do. As soon as they walked out the door I went off on Malcolm. I asked him how long he's been having sex with his babysitter. He stood there looking at me like his father would when he didn't care about my feelings. He calmly said since the first time she came. I asked him if she was the only one and he said no. I screamed "NO???" And then I came after him, he looked surprised. I guess he didn't expect me to care. I didn't expect me to care either.

When I started hitting on him he told me to stop. When I didn't he
pushed me down on the couch. He seemed so big as he stood over
me visibly angry and like he was battling with himself about
hitting me. "You will not hit me! Anymore! I am not your
punching bag!" No he didn't! This is my child, right or wrong he
will not disrespect me in my house. I started swinging again. I
called him every black beast and creature I could think of.
Malcolm got up and went in his room. I followed him in his room
still cursing him, hitting him, saying stuff like his father took one
look at his black skin and left us because of him. Malcolm grabbed
his pajama pants to put on over his shorts, and sneakers. I ran then
I blocked the front door telling him he wasn't leaving. Malcolm's
eyes turned black and he told me if I didn't move he was going to
move me. I stood against the door and folded my arms. Malcolm
exhaled and walked like he was going back in his room. Then he
started running at me, he jumped and kicked me in my chest. I fell
in front of the door. So he popped the screen out of the window
next to the door and climbed out. He knocked the wind out of me
and it took a minute to recover. When I got up my chest hurt, but I
walked across the courtyard to Melanie's. I knew Malcolm ran over
here telling her all my business. I pounded on the door. Troy
opened the door and Melanie was sitting on the couch looking at
me. I asked them if Malcolm was there, and they both held the
same confused expression. Troy ran and grabbed his shoes and
jacket. Melanie asked him where he was going and he said to go
find Malcolm. I ran behind Troy. When he realized I was
following him he ran faster. It was dark and it was cold. I realized
we were heading towards my momma's house and I started running
harder. When I rounded the corner the porch light was on and her
front door just closed. I ran harder, the door was locked. Fuzzy
opened the door and everybody in the house was waking up.
Malcolm had tears running down his face and he was still mad.
"What happened?" Momma asked Malcolm with her hand on his

back as she rubbed it.

"YOU WILL NOT HIT ME ANYMORE!" He yelled at me. "ALL SHE DOES IS HIT ME, CALL ME NAMES, GET HIGH, AND SLEEP AROUND!"

I rolled my eyes, "and you came over here for sympathy? Where you think I got it from?"

"He could've killed you, what do you think I'm training them for?"

"He's not supposed to use that crap on me!"

"On anyone who's a threat to him, why would you be special?" Macio's voice vibrated off the walls.

"I'm his momma!"

"He's barely with you. He might as well stay here momma. He can sleep in my room on the floor. Anything would be better for him than living with you."

"Fine! But who's gonna pay for him?" Momma asked like we were talking about a puppy.

"He's gonna pay for himself. He got a job."

"And he cut my hair earlier. He can do that on the side." Fuzzy volunteered.

Tears filled my eyes, "Fuzzy?" How could he turn on me like this?

"Pam, you are worse than my momma. At least she left, I mean that hurt. But it would hurt more if she was here doing me like you do him. You are the worst momma!"

"Fuzzy!" Everybody was looking at me with evil eyes. "I'm not worse than momma!"

"I know I have my ways, but you're all that boy got and look at how you act." My momma said.

"I'm not worse than YOU!"

She smiled and folded her arms. "Prove it! Who's his daddy?"

I slumped, I couldn't tell the truth whether Eugene denies me or not. "I say that man is. What's his name?" She snapped her fingers trying to remember. I wasn't going to help her. "You know who I'm talking about. Your sister says you slept with her man. There was the kid from your father's place, and then the supposed boyfriend that only one person ever barely saw. Tell the truth for once in your life!"

"You're not asking cause you care about me or him. You're hoping there's money to be had behind knowing the truth. It don't matter who his father is, he don't want him no how. Just leave it blank."

My momma got mad, probably cause I had her number. She started charging at me. I ran out the door. Momma told me not to come back.

Chapter 6

I exhaled and looked at the bottom of my glass. "Is this watered down? It tastes good, but I'm not feeling anything."

"I find it interesting how you're glazing over the things you did to Malcolm. You will get no sympathy from me. I know how to read between the lines. The stuff you're saying shifts timelines and doesn't add up." I could see his disregard for my lies in his eyes. "You know Moses works for Malcolm now."

"Tell Malcolm to get away from him! He has to know Moses is plotting on him!" I got nervous. "He...."

"Malcolm doesn't need you to figure anything out for him. He's on top of it."

"I'm not worse than my momma. I never pimped Malcolm out."

"Is that supposed to lessen the things you did do?"

"I know it was wrong to beat on him. I know I had no right to talk about him the way I did."

"You never showed him human decency!"

"But my momma did?"

"Why you let your brother keep him when you know he was the one introducing Malcolm to sex and everything else? Then you wanna get mad when he's acting on the things he was taught."

"It was his so what attitude about the whole thing. He was a little boy he should've been getting butterflies from holding hands. Not digging out girls more than twice his age."

"What example did you set for him contrary to that?"

"That don't matter, no parent should walk in on their child having sex."

"You were barely out of jail. You spent more time in than out. Why are you glossing over that?"

"Who told you?" He didn't respond he stared. "Stuff kept happening and coming up. It wasn't my fault that I kept ending up in there." He stared at me like he didn't believe me.

If I wanted something and I didn't have the money to buy I'd take it. Most times I was fine as long as I didn't take Jodi or her stupid boyfriend. Jodi would beg cause she needed the help. We both had habits we needed to support by any means necessary.

~

Anyways, I had just gotten out of the shower and I couldn't put my finger on why the thought of Malcolm's empty room bothered me. There was a strong knock at the door. I looked out the window and my heart fluttered it was Eugene. I opened the door in only my towel. Eugene grinned at my towel. "Why haven't you called me?"

"It's been a lot going on. I didn't have the energy."

He frowned, "you didn't have the energy to call me?" He looked around, "what did I tell you about smoking?"

I put my hand on my hip. "You haven't been around, and if you were my only reason not to...."

"You shouldn't want to do it for yourself. Smoking leads to other stuff."

"No it doesn't!"

He looked at me, "look at you. You've got habits that cigarettes only pacify until you can get to the next thing."

"That's me, that's not a rule!"

"Well I'm only talking about you." Then he looked around. "Your boy a hard sleeper why you so loud?"

"He's not here."

"Where is he?"

"Like you care!"

He squinted his eyes at me. "I asked you didn't I? Don't piss me off."

"Or else what? You gonna stop coming by? Been there done that!"

"Where is he?"

"At my momma's."

He sat on the couch, "how old is he now?"

"He'll be nine in June."

"Time flies don't it?" He smiled at me. "I saw your sister."

"So!" I tried to act unconcerned.

He started laughing. "She got heck of kids!"

"Why is that funny?"

"Cause she was constantly talking about she was better than you. Then she the one having baby after baby confusing sex for love. At least you get paid; she's getting stuck with the bill with those kids. That little chubby one look just like you if you was chubby."

"Bernadette is my brother's daughter and she's pretty, but I don't understand why you think you can sit here talking about Belle to me. You the one who started her on her bad habit in the first place. You pumped her head up, made her think sex meant love. You created that monster."

"Then why you only have one?"

"If you wouldn't have done what you did I wouldn't have that one. I don't want the one I got."

"Here we go, you know that's my father's baby. I don't know how you think pinning him on me is going to help you. I told you, you need to show him to my father."

"Why hasn't he asked to see him?"

"When I see my father we discuss business. I don't have nothing to tell him. And I told you, I'm denying all charges."

My feelings were so hurt. "You left me because of the baby you gave me."

"That is not my son, I told you that."

"Then why are you here?"

He leaned back and put his feet up on my coffee table. "You know why?"

I blew air, "I'm not in the mood! Get out!"

"Is this about money? I'll pay you, you're worth it." He winked at me.

"Get out!"

He grumbled then he stood up. "Why? I don't want to leave."

"I'm in love with you! Belle moved on with her life and you still treat me like a second class hooker..."

"No you're first class!"

"Get out! I can't do this with you. I haven't seen you in years and you only come back to remind me of the pain I've been running from for all these years."

"You sure you want me to leave?" He looked down at me.

"I didn't stutter!"

Eugene left and I threw myself on the bed. I cried myself to sleep, I was depressed I had no money and I could use a fix right now. Even if it's just grass, anything to take my mind off all of this.

****

It was morning and I rolled over trying to think of anything other than Eugene. I cleaned up, dressed, and then I started walking. I was wandering around aimlessly.

I sat across the street watching the kids on the playground playing. When it was time Belle walked up to the school gathering her kids and hugging them all. I never hug Malcolm, I'm so mad at him. Why he have to be so black? It's not fair! He's the reason Eugene stopped loving me and completely changed up on me.

Troy waived goodbye to Belle then he and Malcolm started walking. They were about twenty feet away when a group of girls came running up to them. They were all giggly about Troy and paying Malcolm no attention. Malcolm walked on the side while these girls circled Troy. He said something and the girls one by one hugged Troy and waived bye barely at Malcolm. They walked on to the deli.

There was a fancy car in the parking lot closest to the deli with a driver standing and waiting. Malcolm and Troy looked at the car then they went inside. I sat across the street watching. Eventually Rita's father and a big white man walked out talking. The big man got in the back of his car and left. Rita's father came out a few minutes later telling her he'd be back. As he was leaving Fuzzy and Leonard walked up.

Rita gave all the boys instruction, she smiled at Malcolm. I shifted my weight from leg to leg trying to understand what I was feeling. She was talking to Malcolm and she kept touching him, I didn't like it. Then out of nowhere my momma came storming over there kicking up a fuss. Knowing my momma whatever it was it had to do with money. My momma was fussing and the boys were doing their best to stand down.

For whatever reason there was nothing neither she nor Macio could do to turn those four against each other. There's other cousins their ages who they interact with, etc. but it's always the four of them. It may seem like my momma leaves them alone, but I know better. I know how she always put us up against each other she ain't changed. Momma grabbed Malcolm's arm like she was going to take him away. He snatched his arm back and stood planted. My momma was yelling at him and she raised her hand like she was going to hit him and even across the way I could see the look he gave her. My momma paused then she went back to fussing. I guess Macio's words replayed in her mind when he told me Malcolm could've killed me. I don't know business, but this scene in front of their store can't be a good idea. Why would she try to get them fired?

Troy went into peacekeeping mode. He got my momma to walk back to her car with him. Leonard stood next to Malcolm watching my momma walk away. Sometimes I wonder if someone told them they're brothers and they don't let us in on it. Leonard patted Malcolm on the back and then he went back to work.

Then as if he knew I followed them Malcolm turned towards me and stared. I was so busy staring back that I didn't notice Fuzzy until he grabbed me to scare me. I screamed and he laughed. My nephew has gotten so big! That little baby was now in his teenage body taller than me, and bigger than me in every way. He laughed at my scream then he asked me what I wanted. I shook my head to say nothing; I didn't know what I wanted so how could I tell him. He pointed at Malcolm who turned and walked inside. He said Malcolm was getting big and I agreed. He said with the way he carried his self older girls always breaking their necks to get at him. They never believe him when he says how young he is. I asked why he doesn't hold hands with girls his age. Fuzzy laughed and said Malcolm needed more than holding hands and little girls his age always get hung up on his color. Fuzzy said he swears Malcolm gets more play just because he's so dark. I thought about Whispers and I did see him because he was so dark. I don't know why it's ok for Whispers to be black, but I hated it on my son! I wondered what happened to Whispers. After all these years would he still look at me like I was worth anything? Sometimes I look in the mirror and I wonder where I went. Some men still act like I'm pretty, but I know the difference.

I asked him what my momma wanted. He said he told Leonard not to buy those new shoes. He said Leonard needed new shoes cause his had a hole in the bottom. As soon as she noticed his shoes she knew they were holding out on her. She was trying to make them talk, she tried to sick Macio on them. He smiled so big when he said Macio's face was priceless when he realized he needed to stand down or they would kill him. He said they all handover their regular money from the deli every Friday. He said Rita's father pays them extra to keep the deli and Rita secure when he leaves. I asked him where her father goes and he smiled and said he takes care of business. I asked him if it was good money and he smiled. I asked him why she grabbed Malcolm. He said she be forgetting that he's the worst one. Then he looked at me and said I was the only person who got away with hitting him and Malcolm had enough. Not that I cared but I asked Fuzzy if Malcolm hated me. He said he thinks Malcolm should but he doesn't talk about me. Shocked I asked him why he thought Malcolm should. He said because he knew for fact that I'm capable of being better to people than I ever was to my own son. He said even Belle was a better momma than me. That hurt cause she always has hated me. He said Momma Shuga basically took Leonard once he started working at the deli. He said Belle came over crying about it. Momma Shuga beat her, then she told her she couldn't afford to feed him and she owed her since she never put in work for her momma. I asked him if she took Troy too? I don't see Melanie around too much whenever I am home. He said she tried but Melanie wasn't having it and neither was Troy. I exhaled and then I hugged Fuzzy I thanked him for talking to me.

****

"What are you going to do when you get out?" The woman asked in a tender voice that made my skin crawl.

"Check in at the shelter and try to find out about my stuff. You think they sold it all?"

"It is highly unlikely that your landlord held on to your things. Look at it as an opportunity to start over fresh with a brand new start."

I started crying hard, "I don't want to start over. Eugene bought all that furniture for me, all except the bed. Before then nobody had ever bought me nothing. I want my stuff back! All those memories gone! It don't matter to nobody but me."

The woman gave me tissues for my face. "Pamela I know you're upset, but maybe this is for the best. You keep coming back here for ridiculous things. Maybe one day you can start building a life for yourself. There's more to life than going in and out of jail. Fighting, stealing, all this stuff that adds nothing to your life. You need to find your place in the world."

"Maybe I should've never been born! I can't imagine why my momma didn't throw me away. It's not like she's ever showed anybody any love outside of my daddy and Macio."

"Can you try talking to her? Maybe you'll be surprised to find out how much she does love you."

I shook my head at the memory. "I was trying to talk to her one time. I was asking her hard questions and she was getting madder and madder at me. But I was trying like my life depended on it." I clinched my lips, "Malcolm came in interrupting us. I hit him and told him to get out. She beat me up claiming she didn't appreciate the way I was treating him. If I didn't get it before, I got it then. She doesn't want to answer questions about anything."

She cut her eyes at me. "You hit your son for interrupting? Children interrupt, that's what they do."

"I don't want to argue about this. If abortion was legal when I got pregnant, he wouldn't be here. I know enough about myself to know I'm not mother material. It's not like my momma was a good mother. You know some of my sisters, I'm not saying anything they haven't said."

The woman sat there clearly irritated with me. "You know while you're cursing your fertility there are women who would give anything to be in your shoes. To be able to carry life and to take it for granted is not something that every woman is blessed with. Some of us will never know the feeling of feeling life grow from within. Bringing that precious life into the world and watching it grow into something great. You...."

"Great? From me? From my family? We're just a bunch of niggas.

Born niggas, and we gonna die niggas. Bringing another life into this messed up world is selfish! All that child will know is pain, neglect, and disappointment! Don't matter how good of a parent anyone is. All it takes is one person to selfishly rob them of their innocence or worse their life and it's over! Fertility is not a blessing it's a curse that's passed on."

The lady started crying, she put her forehead in the palm of her hand as she shook her head and cried. That's what she gets for trying to make me feel anything. She tried to calm down but she couldn't. She had to walk away and someone else came to finish my exit interview.

I checked in at the shelter and then I went to my old apartment. The apartment manager was different and he had no clue as to what I was talking about. Melanie didn't even live here anymore. I sat across the street from the deli waiting and watching hoping that the boys still worked here. I watched the cars that passed and then Malcolm's voice jarred me. "When did you get out?" He stared at me like he was searching for something in my eyes.

"This morning."

"What do you want?"

"Melanie moved, I need to talk to her."

"Why?" He asked completely removed from me.

"Maybe she kept something from our old place before they threw everything away."

"It's not like you could fit the clothes."

I pulled on my shirt that was a little snug. I've gained so much weight recently, I don't know why. "Thank you for that, I guess I wouldn't have noticed if you didn't point it out. Actually, I was hoping she had at least one piece of furniture from there."

"Leave my aunt alone."

I frowned, "I'm not going to hurt Melanie."

"She moved, that's all you need to know."

Malcolm was still black, still my biggest mistake. He has the nerve to stand here talking to me like he's lost his mind. "You would think at some point you'd start getting lighter. You couldn't possibly get any darker."

He squinted at me and I wanted to hit him. "I hurt your feelings by protecting her don't I?"

"Yes!"

"Good! Now wobble your fat behind on! You're disgusting!"

"I can wait for Troy."

"We don't let people loiter around here. You better be happy I recognized you otherwise you'd be dead. I don't care where you go but you can't stay here."

"Loiter? What that mean? I want to see Troy!"

"You want to go get some exercise and get some clothes that actually fit you."

"Everything ok?" Another kid I didn't know asked.

"Yes, she was just leaving."

"Who are you?"

"Jason ma'am."

"She's not a ma'am or anyone you'd ever need to assign respect to." Malcolm said matter of factly.

"Malcolm!" I couldn't believe him.

Jason looked at Malcolm then me. "Ma'am you better leave, and fast." He gently grabbed my arm. "You go ahead and go inside, I'll walk her to the corner." He told Malcolm who stood there staring. I guess he looked angry but how could you tell?

"Who are you?" I asked after we took a few steps away.

"Leonard is my best friend, and it looks like an angel sent me to save you. He's not someone you want to get on their bad side ever."

"Do you know where Troy is?" He looked at me but didn't respond. I searched his eyes for kindness but I didn't see it. I exhaled and walked on.

~

 "STOP! You're always lying! Now you're trying to say that's how you met Jason?" The guy asked like he knew for a fact my timeline was off.

"Just listen, it will make sense in a minute." My hands sweated a little. Who is this guy? How he going to tell me as if he knows otherwise about MY FAMILY? I continued on with my story…

~

I found myself at my momma's house. Macio was outside with the little ones drilling them as usual. I could hear my momma fussing and carrying on inside. When I stepped in the door Fuzzy was standing there looking like a man, not the teenager I saw not too long ago. "Grandma, I'm only moving around the corner. There's no room for us here. We will be here everyday."

"If you take Leonard, Malcolm is going to want to go, and that's not going to happen."

"We've already talked it out. Malcolm is going to stay. Provided that you keep people out of his room."

My momma looked at me. "When did you get out?"

"This morning."

"You got fat!"

"Gee thanks momma! I didn't notice."

She sucked her teeth. "What good are you supposed to be to anyone looking like that?"

Does that mean she thinks she can't pimp me looking like this? Internally I smiled. "I don't know. Where can I find Melanie?"

"What you want with her?"

The only way she'll help me is if it's drama related. "She was telling the neighbors my business and I haven't forgotten."

Momma stared at me for a minute. "You need to stop smoking and all that other crap, it's affecting your looks. You're too young to be looking so old."

Renee came out the bathroom pregnant belly, hair wild all over her head, and it looked like she had been crying. She looked at Fuzzy with sad eyes and he looked away. She looked at me and sucked her teeth. "When did you get out?"

"What happened to your hair?"

"Lavonia."

"Who's that?"

"Macio's girlfriend!" She clinched her teeth and looked out the door. "Anybody tell you they found my momma's body?"

"No, when was the funeral?" I looked at my momma.

"Funeral?" Renee huffed and looked at my momma. "The only person who's ever got a funeral around here has been her husband. She don't care about none of us!"

"Shut up! Nobody cares that you were born and no one will care when you die. Funerals are for the living. And I'm not wasting my money on that junk."

Fuzzy was all over the place. "Bye! It's done! You know where we are." Then he stormed out the door. He headed towards a car.

"Fuzzy! Can I get a ride downtown to the shelter?" I asked.

"Come on." He got in his car.

I got in and looked around. "This is a nice car."

He cut his eyes at me. "Auntie stay away from her, protect yourself cause I can't protect you from her and Malcolm won't."

"He hate me or something?"

"He don't talk about you, but he don't stop anybody else from talking about you either."

"I guess I deserve that. How's he doing?"

"He's blazing through school. He goes to middle school next year. Someone told them chess was a thinkers game and the three of them been playing ever since."

"He still works at the deli though."

"How you know?"

"I went there first."

"He works at the deli but he don't work at the deli."

"What does that mean?"

"What I just said. You need to stay away from Momma Shuga. She has been money hungry these days. Tricey left but she left her kids here. Lon and Jan did the same thing. She broke Belle down and she finally put her out."

"What about Melanie?"

"Please Auntie Melanie can only deal with Troy. She falls apart about everything else."

"Who is Lavonia?"

"Macio's crazy girlfriend. She convinced Momma Shuga to let her show her how well she can do hair. Talking about she wanted to do all her trick's hair. Renee was her tester and you see her hair. It was funny watching her beat her up though. She put that stuff on Renee's hair it burned her. They washed it out. She call herself styling it. When she gave Renee the mirror." He smiled real big, "Renee calmly put the mirror down and then she beat that girl up all over the house." Fuzzy laughed, "it was heck of funny!" Fuzzy talked and laughed all the way to the shelter. I mostly listened to him; I couldn't believe how big he's gotten. I started wondering what Leonard and Troy looked like. I thanked Fuzzy for the ride then he touched my arm before I got out. "Pam!" He exhaled, "why do you do what she tells you to do? Momma Shuga don't mean nobody no good."

I knew he was right. "I know baby, that's my momma."

"She got my momma killed and doesn't care. I can't live in her house! The only reason I'm cordial is for Malcolm's sake."

"What do you mean?"

"She holds on to him for dear life even more than Macio. Malcolm and Macio came to blows, and the only reason Macio's still here is because Troy calmed Malcolm down. Momma Shuga provoked that whole situation. Once she saw that Malcolm was stronger and smarter she's been giving him whatever he wants to keep him around. As long as there's something in it for her of course. Malcolm and Macio made up eventually to a point but now they don't trust each other where they used to be like father and son. Macio used to say Malcolm was his Michael."

"His who?"

"Macio is probably the biggest Jackson 5 fan. He'd have us dancing like we were them and we better had got the steps right." Fuzzy smiled.

I started cracking up, "dancing? Really? All of you?"

Fuzzy chuckled, "ok, ok. I'll admit that his crazy was kind of fun when it came to that. Smoke the only one who can sing, but Macio said Malcolm had to be Michael cause he's the littlest."

"Oh what I wouldn't give to have seen you guys dancing. So you guys can dance. Wow!" I guess I kept laughing too long, cause Fuzzy sat there no longer smiling. I couldn't escape the vision of the five of them dancing and trying to sing. Or that Malcolm could ever be on the level of little chocolate Michael. He's burnt crispy black. My brother is completely off.

Fuzzy exhaled, then he started talking. "I'm cordial because I need access to that house if anything happens. Malcolm says she's not that crazy cause she's been enjoying the money he's been bringing in. I remind him that my momma is dead because of a trick she sent her on knowing the situation wasn't cool. She got Renee out there and a lot of the cousins." Then he looked at me, "if she hears of any of this I will know it came from you. I'll forget you're my auntie."

I frowned, "boy! Don't you ever threaten me!"

"Your boy ain't here! You better remember that I'm a man now. If it wasn't for the kindness you showed me when I was young I'd treat you like I treat the rest of those lying tricks around there. I don't like your life. And I HATE the way you treat my little cousin. I've lost all respect for you!"

"Fuzzy, I..."

"You act like he had some choice over the color of his skin. You shouldn't have laid with his father if his color bothers you so much."

"His father isn't dark like that!"

"That light skinned man is not his father!"

"What do you want me to say?"

Fuzzy stared disappointedly at me. "If you don't know I don't know what to tell you." He shook his head, "it's a shame though. As big as our family is nobody can work together. We're the grandkids you all are a bunch of disappointments. Get out!"

"Because of Malcolm?"

"Because of you! Get out!"

~

I shook my head as tears fell. That was one of the most painful conversations I've ever had in my life.

"Even when you know you're about to die you still won't tell the truth? What does it matter to you?" He looked so irritated.

"Stop interrupting me!" I slurred a little, I guess something was starting to take affect.

Chapter 7

"I have to pee!" I was lying.

"Piss on yourself, it's not like you need to be clean where you're going." He didn't care.

"I'm not going to pee on myself. That's disgusting!"

"You're disgusting!"

"I'm not an animal."

"That's a matter of opinion."

I looked around the naked walls hoping something would show me how to get out of here.

~

I got a job at the pizza joint downtown not too far from the halfway house I was at. My job was to make the pizzas, put them in the oven, box them up, and give them to the customer with the right receipt. It's very rare that I paid attention to the customers. I didn't love my job, but it was cool. I liked getting a paycheck though. "Number 89?" I called out.

As I lifted the box he said, "Pam?"

It was Archie! I immediately felt self-conscious about my appearance. I was hot, sweating, and not cute at all. "Number 89?" I called out.

"That's me."

"Cheese and peppers?"

"Pam?"

"Look! I'm at work! Cheese and peppers? Napkins or plates?"

He looked mad, "daddy who's that?" A little girl asked him.

I went back to work. I didn't wait to hear his explanation. He's married and she doesn't need to worry about who I am. I don't look the same and I know it. I saw Eugene on the street, he walked right past me without recognizing me, and he didn't even look back at me with any recognition. The woman on his arm was beautiful, and he still looks like chocolate silk. I was heart achingly depressed for weeks about it. This is who I am now oh well.

On my off days from work I'd battle with the idea of going to see my family. I wonder about Malcolm sometimes he's gotten so tall and solid; his voice was always deep even when he was little. I wonder if it's cracking now or if it ever did. Thinking about him makes me feel weird so I normally change the station in my mind. I was sitting on the front step smoking my cigarette when I saw Archie approaching, I said a curse then I put my cigarette out. When he got close I asked him how he found me. He said somebody around the corner at my job told him I lived here. I asked him what he wanted. He frowned and asked me why I wasn't happy to see him. I told him I didn't understand why he would think I'd be happy about a married man coming to see me. He said he was going to get a divorce. He said they weren't a good match. Then he asked me where Malcolm was. I pushed past the tears that wanted to come forward and I said he was with my momma. He asked me when he could see him cause he knew he had to be really big by now. I asked him why he wanted to see him. He said he wanted to see his son. I blank stared at him. He said Malcolm always felt like he was his when he held him. I told him if that were true then he abandoned us. He told me to stop being difficult and to get up and hug him. When I didn't move he made me stand up and he hugged me tight. I tried not to like it or feel like I needed this. This was my first gentle intentional touch in years. I didn't like how good it made me feel. He wasn't going to get me strung out on the feeling. I backed up and I asked him what he wanted. He simply said he wanted me. That made me mad and I screamed at him. He stood there looking at me like he was letting me get it out and he could wait for it to be over. When I stopped to catch my breath he asked me if I wanted to go get something to eat. I reluctantly said yes. Archie told me to go get my purse. When I looked in the mirror my face was shining and I didn't look anything like I wanted to look. I washed my face, braided my Afro down into two braids, and changed my shirt. Then I looked in the mirror again. It was better, but I could do better. I borrowed my roommate's earrings and put on gloss. That's when I noticed that my complexion was lifeless. I've been good not touching any drugs since I've been out. I guess these cigarettes weren't helping me either. I told myself I could go the evening without needing another one. I pulled at my shirt and then I felt defeated. Who am I kidding? I look nothing like my old self. I know how pretty I used to be. The reflection staring back at me is not who I am. Or maybe my true self is finally showing. I was my prettiest after I gave birth. I had that amazing woman's body. Eugene really couldn't get enough back then. Now my curves are just roundness and FACE! Where did I go? I don't really care about my weight but my beautiful face! I miss it! I plopped on my bed too depressed to go out there and face Archie.

My roommate walked in the room right as I started crying. "Are those my earrings?"

"I was borrowing them, I was going to give them back."

"What's wrong with you?"

"I looked in the mirror."

"And?"

"I'm not pretty anymore!"

"No you're not, but what do you mean by anymore?" She smiled, "haven't you always looked this beastly?"

I gasped then I started laughing. "No! I used to be really pretty."

"What happened?"

"Life! Heck if I know! Then the guy who's always been after me since we were kids shows up wanting to take me out. I can't go out there, not like this."

"He asked you out sight unseen?"

"No, I came in to grab my purse. Then I looked in the mirror."

"If he already saw you why are you melting down? You still got something."

"I guess, I just don't feel pretty."

"A man came and asked you out. If you don't stop you're belly aching! If a man says hi to me I'm liable to give it all away on the spot. Just go enjoy whatever you're going to do. We can continue this bonding moment when you come back with my earrings."

"Ok."

"You should smile more often."

"Ok."

When I walked outside Archie was walking in. He said he thought he was about to have to drag me out. I sat quietly in his car as he talked the entire way to the restaurant. He seemed to be so excited to be with me. When we sat at the table he reached out for my hands and then he happily held them. "Pam, I've missed you."

Embarrassed I dropped my head. "I don't know why."

"I've always been in love with you. How many times did I ask you to marry me?"

"That wasn't real." I kept my head down.

"Yes it was! Why would you have thought I was kidding?"

"Who would ever want to marry me?"

"I do!"

"You mean did."

"I mean do!"

"But you're married."

"We're not together. We're going to get a divorce."

"What happened?"

He said it was all his fault. He had a good woman; she's a good wife and a good mother. I sunk further in my seat, I told him he should make up with his wife. I'd never be a good wife and Malcolm would testify that I'm not a good mother. Archie took me back to his small one bedroom apartment. He showed it with so much pride. Who am I to judge how small it is? I have nowhere, the only way my momma will let me back in her house is if I'm willing to lay on my back for her. She's so mad at me for letting myself go, I doubt even opening my legs would get me back in. I told him his place was nice. He asked me if I wanted to move in. I told him he doesn't even know me. I was the most honest I've ever been when I told him I'm a liar and a thief. I told him I've been good for now but I like taking drugs. Anything that could stop me from existing in this world of pain. I couldn't get comfortable or calm, my body was screaming for my nicotine fix. I begged Archie to take me home. I left my purse as I ran to my pack of cigarettes on the dresser. I ran back outside and oh my goodness it was good! I could think straight again. Archie silently watched me enjoy every inhale on my cigarette. I told him I needed to think about it. He didn't understand what there was to think about but he told me he has to work for the next five days and then he'd come back.

****

"Number fourteen!" I called out. The person cursed and then I noticed my *son* who would've preferred to be looking at anybody else. "Why aren't you at school?"

"Don't worry about it. My pizza..." He reached for it.

"Your pizza?" I snatched the box backwards. "You need to be at school."

Malcolm tilted his head to the side as he looked at me. He started walking along the counter, and then he turned the corner. He entered the kitchen and walked in my face. "Do you want to piss me off right now? I have no tolerance for being hungry." He was a controlled angry.

"Pam? Who is he? He can't be back here!" My coworker said.

"Tell her to give me my food and I'll leave."

Then our manager walked in the kitchen. "Oh no! Pam! Again! What did you do?"

"I didn't do nothing, he should be at school."

"Who are you, his mother? That's a paying customer, give him his food."

"But..."

He cut me off, "I'm about tired of you and the drama with

customers." He turned to Malcolm, "I'm sorry sir. She will bring your pizza out."

"That one is now cold. I like my pizza piping hot without her sweat dripping on it. I need a new fresh one. Tell her to throw in some chicken wings and a salad."

I couldn't believe that the manager was going for this. He reached for the receipt on the pizza. "Number fourteen a fresh pie will be out in a few minutes."

Malcolm squinted at me and my blood boiled. "Make sure you watch her so she don't spit in my food."

The manager looked at me, "she better not!"

Malcolm walked out the kitchen and into the dining room. My manager started busting my chops about everything without even knowing what was going on. And ok so sometimes I argue with customers but he doesn't even know this situation. Of course he wouldn't link Malcolm to me, that black beast knows no one would automatically think we know each other. I wanted to put something in his food or drop it on the floor before serving him. When the food was ready my manager told me to take it to his table with a smile and then he walked behind me. When I walked in the dining room Malcolm, Troy, Leonard, Fuzzy, and a fat guy I didn't recognize were sitting at the table. Malcolm and Leonard held the same expression as they looked at me. They were sitting there looking like their daddy. Only the glare looked worse on Malcolm because everything looks worse on him. "Hey auntie!" Troy said getting up to hug me.

"Why aren't you all at school?"

"Aw! And you said she didn't care!" Troy said with a smile at Malcolm. "How you been? How long you been out?"

"You know him?" The manager asked me.

"They're all my nephews."

"Your family is huge!" Then he turned to them. "Would you like a pitcher of soda?"

"Well if you're offering I don't see why not." Troy said happily.

"Come with me," he said to Troy. "Pam! Get back to work."

"Cool little job." Malcolm said as he flipped me the bird.

I thought I was going to walk away, but I found myself running at him. Malcolm stood up and slapped my head so hard I fell. He stepped on my chest and calmly asked me what I was doing. "Pam!" My manager said with his hands on his hips. "This is your family! I can't have this type of behavior here! You're begging to be fired!"

"Let her up." Troy said reaching for my hand. Malcolm took his foot off my chest and then he stood there watching me. "Be cool auntie, you don't want to lose your job."

Malcolm and I were locked in a stare down. Then I walked to the kitchen. I hung up my apron then I picked up the knife I used to slice the vegetables for the salad. Malcolm was back at the counter when I turned around. He looked at my hand then my face. "I really hope for your sake that's for work. If you're ever stupid enough to come at me with a weapon you better kill me cause I will not hold back! Now give me a couple of boxes, I'm leaving."

I remembered Macio's words and I exhaled. "Why would you disrespect me like this?" I handed him boxes.

"You've never given me anything to respect. Besides, I don't start stuff with you. You hate yourself so much that you used to take that out on me. I told you before; you don't get to hit me anymore. Next time you see me control yourself. Learn how to love yourself enough to value your life."

****

"Archie I'm a mess. You don't want someone like me. Especially around your kids."

"I'm a mess too. Let's be a mess together. My kids will adjust and be fine. Maybe you could bring Malcolm and we could introduce them at the same time."

I laid my head back on the pillow as tears poured out of my eyes. "Malcolm hates me! I can't blame him."

"He doesn't hate you, you're his mother." Archie rubbed my back.

"Yes he does. I'm not a good mother."

"Every parent feels like that. I know you've done something's but he loves you."

"He's the reason his father left me. He took one look at him and dismissed me. My family thinks you're his father."

He smiled real big, "really? That's great! Let's go get Malcolm. It's not too late."

"It is for me and Malcolm. My momma brings women and older girls who've developed some kind of taste around him."

He frowned, "what does that mean?"

"It's very rare that girls Malcolm's age would look at him and see past his burnt blackness. Plus he looks older than he actually is."

"Malcolm's having sex already? Could he have kids?"

I shrugged, "I don't know. He's in the seventh grade, I would hope not."

"Can I try to talk to him?"

"To say what?"

"I was thinking," he cleared his throat. "Hello Malcolm. I'm your father. I'd like you to meet your sisters. Something like that."

"Malcolm is mean, he's not going to go for it."

"Every child wants to know who their father is."

"But you're not his father, Malcolm is smart. He's a different kind of child. He will know it's not the truth."

"How do you know I'm not his father? Maybe the condom broke and I didn't tell you out of fear."

"Look at Malcolm mister light skinned. That boy is darker than night, there's no way you're his father."

"Only me and my sister is light skinned in my family. The rest of them are brown to dark brown. Both of my girls are brown. Why are you so hung up on the color of Malcolm's skin?"

"Because! Until I saw his grandfather I had never in my life seen anyone that black before. It's the first thing out of people's mouths since he was born. Why he gotta be my son looking like that?"

"You think it makes him ugly?"

"YES!"

"I'm sure he's a very handsome young man, he was a good looking kid."

"You've always had stars in your eyes when it came to him. Why are you so obsessed with him?"

"I told you, that's my son. My only son and want him to know me." There was a flicker of something in his eyes.

Something told me it wasn't a good idea. I can't call myself a good mother to even try to say it was a mother's intuition. We've got into so many fight behind him probing about Malcolm. "Archie, I don't think it's a good idea."

He smiled big, "let's go."

"Where?"

"Let's go find him."

"No." I protested.

Archie convinced me, I don't know how, to get up and get dressed. We went to my momma's house. As soon as my momma laid eyes on Archie I knew this was a mistake. She kept staring at Archie like she was looking for a sign of money or something. She told me which middle school to go to, and then she stared.

When we pulled up to the school Fuzzy was waiting in his car. "Archie this is my nephew Fuzzy, Fuzzy this is my boyfriend Archie."

Fuzzy smiled, "I've heard a lot about you." Then he looked at me. "Why are you here?"

"He wants to see Malcolm."

Fuzzy's eyes bounced between us, "why?"

"I believe I could be his daddy."

Fuzzy tried to hold back his smile but he started laughing really hard. A fancy car pulled along the curb in front of our cars. A woman got out her car, she looked at us, nodded, then she walked inside. I recognized her walk and the ring on her finger cause it made me drool the same way it did when I was high that time. We were all staring as she walked inside the school. Fuzzy suggested that we leave but he knew we weren't leaving. I walked up to the fancy car and looked inside and all around it. The insides were clean and the car sparkled like it got a hand wax job almost daily. Archie asked me if I wanted a car like that. I smiled then I said I couldn't imagine driving such a fancy car, and then I walked back to him. The school bell rang and kids started pouring out of the school. Students ran for the buses and others ran to their parent's cars. That lady came out slowly looking through papers as she walked next to a little girl who answered questions as she asked them. The little girl was a lot lighter than her and she had her hair braided in one ponytail. The little girl looked sad unlike the rest of the happy kids coming and going. I guess I was looking pretty hard cause the lady looked up from the papers in her hand and the little girl looked at me. They had the same expression on their faces as they scanned me up and down. Neither one of them smiled. The lady looked at Fuzzy and Archie, then she continued talking to her daughter. They got in their car and drove away. When Malcolm walked out the door he looked at me, Archie, and then the girl walking next to him. He stopped walking and she said something else. Malcolm said something then she happily went back inside the school. Malcolm looked at us like he was analyzing our appearance before we got a chance to say. Archie smiled real big at Malcolm. Malcolm immediately frowned. "Man! Look at how big you've gotten!" Archie said like he was in aw.

Malcolm walked up to us. He looked at me while he pointed with his thumb back at Archie. "Who is he supposed to be?"

"I may be your daddy, I was around when you were a baby."

Malcolm looked at Archie hard then he blank stared at me. "This isn't funny."

"Yes it is!" Fuzzy said cracking up. "Let's go get a snack at Big Buck's. Come on Malcolm."

"Why Big Buck's?" I looked at Fuzzy.

"I love that place. We'll meet you there."

"Or..." Archie stared at Malcolm. "Would you mind riding with me while your mother rides with your cousin?"

Malcolm walked towards Fuzzy's car, "NAW! I'll meet you there."

Fuzzy started laughing, I looked at Archie and I shook my head. "I told you!"

When we pulled into the parking lot, I looked around at all the people there looking for Eugene as if he would be there at that exact moment for no reason. I didn't see Eugene but I saw Leonard and Troy as if they were waiting for us. Archie and I sat on one side of the booth. Fuzzy and Malcolm sat on the other side, while Troy and Leonard sat in the booth behind them facing us. "I was hoping we'd get a moment alone to talk."

Fuzzy and Troy smiled, "we are alone." Malcolm said.

"What's happening here?" Troy asked, "auntie is this your boyfriend?"

"Yes."

"Aw! Good for you! You found somebody to love." Troy smiled.

"He thinks he's Malcolm's daddy." Fuzzy announced.

Leonard and Troy started laughing which made Fuzzy laugh again.

"Why is that so funny?"

"Auntie you know he's not Malcolm's father." Fuzzy said like Archie wasn't there.

Archie and Malcolm kept staring at each other. "It is a possibility. That's all I'm saying." I said.

"Can I please talk to you without the audience?" Archie said.

"I don't know you. I don't know where you came from. I don't know what your agenda is. No."

"Your mother was explaining that things are strained between the two of you. I guess now that I think about it, it probably would've been better if I approached you on my own. My name is Archer Rudd. I've known your mother since I was younger than you are now. I'm acknowledging the fact that it is very possible that I could be your father. I know we look nothing a like, but I think you look a lot like your mother. Which would explain why you and your cousin are light and dark skinned versions of the same face."

Malcolm nodded, "that's one theory. I've heard others."

"I feel a fatherly responsibility towards you. If you ever need anything, anything at all please feel free to reach out to me."

"Do you have her in check?"

All of my nephews smiled, "you know your mother."

"Well that right there is how I know for a fact that you are not my father. But thank you for trying, it's not like anyone else ever has."

"What do you mean?" I asked irritated.

"All I remember is if he told you to jump you jumped. I don't remember a face, or even a voice. I remember his presence though.

I'm not hurting for a fill in. Archie, you'll be doing good to manage her. Don't worry about taking me on."

"You think you've seen your father?" I asked.

"I know I have, I was too little to remember him though."

"How do you know it wasn't me?"

"You too soft."

Archie smiled, "right."

****

"Number fifty-three!" I called out then I looked out into the waiting area. My momma was staring at me standing next to Macio. I gave the customer their pizza. "I'm going on my break!" I told everyone then I walked into the dining room.

No hello or anything cordial my momma went in. She explained that Macio's girlfriend has been stealing from Macio, which means she's been stealing from her. She told me she needed me to come get her. I asked my momma why she didn't do it herself. She said she's too old to be fighting. She said that she and Lavonia got into an argument a little bit ago. Then she showed me her bruised cheek. I told my boss I had to go home and that I had a family emergency as I fell out the door behind them. Macio said he'd handle Archie if he ever looked at me like he thought about raising his hand to me. Funny how whenever I needed to make that call to Macio; somehow he was never home. I put that on my momma though, even if he was there, momma was the one saying he wasn't there. I eventually stopped calling, but I appreciated the fact that he at least told me that. Archie and I don't fight all that much, so it's fine I guess.

When we pulled up to the house Renee was arguing with Lavonia in the yard. Lavonia had on a big and long coat and it wasn't really cold but I didn't think anything about it. Malcolm and my nephews were sitting on the porch watching. Lavonia started yelling at my momma calling her all out of her name. Telling her she didn't care who she went to go get my momma needed to stay out of her business. I heard somebody say "OOH!" As I marched up to Lavonia and hit her so hard that it looked like her head almost spun completely around. Everyone said, "OOH!" Again as she went down I jumped on her showing no mercy. Lavonia was screaming as she kept trying to reach for her pocket. I kept hitting her hands in between punches to the face thinking she had a knife. The police came around the corner and I was distracted for a moment. Really quick she pulled out a gun and shot at my momma. Macio grabbed momma and they fell to the ground. I thought she shot my momma and no one could make me stop. I hit the gun out of her hands and I wouldn't stop beating on her. The officers told me to stop but I couldn't. They hit me with something. When they sat Lavonia up she started screaming. Macio's body was convulsing on the ground and my momma was holding on to him screaming "No! No! No!" Everyone on the porch was frozen as they watched. The kids in the house were screaming and carrying on, on the other side of the window. They threw me in one car and they put Lavonia in another. I couldn't stop crying as I looked at my brother's lifeless body on the ground. When they finally took me to the holding cell, I guess they didn't think about the fact that they were putting me in the same holding cell they had Lavonia in. I used the cement walls, the metal bars, and the toilet all as weapons to hurt her as badly as I could. They separated us by moving her banged up body.

****

"Archie wants me to stay away from you guys when I get out." Tears fell down my face.

His glare burned me. "You didn't even know what you were fighting for. And regardless was it worth it?"

"No," I hung my head.

"Momma Shuga don't mean none of y'all no good."

"You think you're different Malcolm?"

"She saved me from you!"

"At what cost?"

"Nothing I can't afford to pay." Then his eyes looked me over. "Look! I've been thinking and I need a straight answer from you. Who's my father?"

A heat wave hit my body, "it doesn't matter."

"If I'm asking, it matters."

I sucked my teeth, "I can't! Malcolm I can't!"

His angry expression didn't change. "You won't tell me to protect yourself. I'm asking for a reason."

"Why? Where's this coming from?"

"You started this, you brought that pathetic excuse to me. Did you tell him that he's my father?"

"Why don't you believe that he could be your father?"

Malcolm's patience was growing thin. "Look at me and then look at him. That man is nothing to me."

"He's loved you since I told him I was pregnant."

Malcolm tilted his head as he watched me. "He actually cares about you? Why?"

Irritation burned in my stomach. "I'm unlovable?" Malcolm blank stared at me like that was a dumb question. "Why are you here? You looking for some kind of bonding moment? I can't stand the look of you!"

"There's the Pam I know. Go ahead and tell me how ugly I am for old times sake."

I stared at him for a minute. I mean I know he's not ugly, but that black skin is the first thing I see, and it makes me mad. That black skin is what made his daddy run. "Why are you here?"

Malcolm took a deep breath, "Macio's gone!" His voice rumbled the table. "You know your momma. The only real family I have are my family, my brothers. Your momma makes it hard with everyone else. I was hoping for once in your life you could be straight with me. Looks like you're still too twisted to do anything right. Next time you get out, do yourself a favor and think for yourself. Stop doing Momma Shuga's dirty work for her."

****

I swallowed hard as I looked at him. I hadn't seen him since that night. He didn't speak; his eyes ran over me like he was trying to remember me. Am I that forgettable that he didn't remember me? "Hello."

"Hello," his eyes still searched me. "You don't look familiar."

I exhaled and ran my hand over my head. "I look that different?"

He squinted his eyes, "Pam? The little girl?"

"That's me."

"What happened to you?"

"Life!"

He looked so disappointed. "You shouldn't be in here."

"Yes I should. I tried to kill that girl. She was aiming for my momma and she got my brother instead. Besides this isn't my first time in here. Why are you here?"

"Your son," he stared at me. "You named him Malcolm. Is he my son?"

I started crying, "I don't know. Eugene insists that he's yours. It's not impossible that he could be yours he looks more like you than he does me or Eugene."

"That doesn't mean he's not Eugene's. I got a grand daughter with my same beautiful coloring. She's the most beautiful little girl I've ever seen. How do you not know?"

"I was with you that night, and then the next night I was unprotected with Eugene."

"How old is he? You can't tell by looking at him."

"He'll be fifteen in June."

Whispers looked around, "I'm not his father."

"He looks just like us."

"Look past his coloring. He looks like you and Eugene. Besides, I got myself fixed almost seventeen years ago. I have too many kids."

I started crying, "does Eugene know that?"

"Probably, it's not like we have these in-depth conversations about our lives. It's not like he even approached me about this kid. Someone else did." He exhaled, "he's pretty impressive."

"Malcolm?"

"Yes Malcolm. Why do you say that like you don't agree or something?"

"What's so impressive about him? He's just a little thug."

He drummed his fingers on the table. "Just a little thug? How do you see your son?"

"He's always plotting, he's bad, and he's disrespectful."

"That must be reserved for you. He's never come at any of my men that way."

"Your men?"

"Your son is analytical, he's cautious, and reserved. He's very smart, he's the baby of their square and he explains it to the rest of them. Your son and nephews have the attention of my employer. If he keeps on like he has he's gonna be running things."

"Has anyone told you Leonard is your grandson as well?"

He was quiet for a minute. He exhaled hard, "I don't know what's wrong with my son. I never denied him!"

"I think he's mad about the time he didn't have with you. He hates his stepfather."

Whispers looked at me, "he told you all that? He tell you about all the time he tried to run from the fact that he's just like me? He's got kids all over the place, but he judges me."

"He denies Malcolm."

"Why?"

"He took one look at him and said he was your baby. Malcolm came here a few months ago asking who his father is. My momma wanna know to hopefully get some money."

"You told him you didn't know?"

"No, I didn't tell him anything."

"Why?"

"Eugene was with my sister, Leonard's momma all that time. It..."

"What does that have to do with Malcolm, and Leonard for that matter? Those boys have no idea they're actually brothers?" I shook my head no. "Pam! This is bigger than you and your sister. They need to know!"

I shook my head, "my sister will lose it and think she's right about every horrible thing she's ever thought about me. Eugene will be mad at me for ever saying anything."

"You don't even talk to Eugene any more."

"Still!"

He looked at me for a long time without speaking. "You deny ever sleeping with me don't you?"

"HUH?" I looked at the table.

"Your sister, what was her name?" He snapped his fingers as he jogged his memory. "Something with an L..." I knew of course but I wasn't saying. "Anyways, you let her bully you into denying me! I chose you first! Why you feel like you gotta hide what you really want?"

Whispers' words laid heavy on my chest. "Because if I ever show that I want something it's taken from me. I'm used to watching for what other people want and taking it from them. It's easier to be the taker."

"So... You push your son away because you're afraid to want him?"

It felt like I couldn't breathe. "Stop!" I cried harder.

"Pam, look at you! Your life is a mess. I offered you better and you chose to slither around with my son. You have an amazing son, and you made it impossible for him to love you." He gestured with his hands around the room. "You're in here, caged in like an animal." He waited for me to get it together enough to look at him. "What happened to the beautiful little girl I used to know? Your beauty was yours and yours alone. You let them push you out of it."

"Shut up!"

"Do you think if you look like this people will forget about you? I didn't even recognize you. What did you do to my beautiful little girl?" I got up and started to walk away, I couldn't even talk. "Pam!" I looked at him. "I'm telling the boys. However you and my ridiculous son choose to deal with it I don't care. They need to know!"

Chapter 8

His walkie-talkie chirped. "Status?" It was my son!

The guy looked at me. "She's babbling on."

"Anything of interest?"

"Ambiguous laments of manipulation."

"Is she coherent?"

"Surprisingly."

"Keep me informed."

"Over," then he put the walkie-talkie back in his jacket.

"If you let me go right now to find my way to the hospital. I promise I'd use a fake name. I will disappear, neither Malcolm nor anyone else would ever know. Please!"

"And when someone comes looking for a body?"

"You already buried me, and by the time they try to dig me up you can disappear."

"Why would I become a liar for you?"

"Because when I woke up this morning I woke up with the thought I was going to live. That I was going to continue on a better path. I have grandchildren I've never really met. A son I need to talk to, to clear the air. Please!"

"So then you don't plan on going away. The reasons you're asking to spare your life are the reasons you could cost me mine for freeing you. Just stop talking! Let the pills do their job and go to sleep."

"I can't stop talking! If I stop talking I'm afraid I will get sleepy!"

~

Archie kissed me and then he squeezed me tight. "Baby I've missed you so much!"

I hugged Archie tightly back. "I missed you too!"

"Tomorrow night the girls are coming and they're going to make you dinner."

"Both of them?" I was surprised cause Archie's oldest did not like me. She had it in her little mind that I was the reason her parents weren't together.

"Yes, I've had a few conversations with them while you were away. We've been open and honest about a lot of things. If they don't like you this time it's on you."

Archie went inside a restaurant and brought lunch out for us. He moved into a bigger place. He said I motivated him to have something better for us when I got out. I liked this house better than his one bedroom apartment, but he could've brought me home to a closet and I would've been happy. He proudly showed me around the two-bedroom house. The house wasn't huge, but I was so thankful to have someone to go home to and to be with someone who cared. Archie jokingly asked me why I lost weight. I was never close to my former post pregnancy weight, but I was now a more manageable size. I felt good about my appearance cause most of the weight left my face. I felt kind of pretty again and that's all I cared. Archie's reaction to me made me feel like the most beautiful woman in the world.

When the girls came over they kept staring at me. They didn't say much, but at least they weren't plotting my death.

****

I got a job at a dry cleaners. I would sort each customer's belongings and put them in the line of clothes to be cleaned. Every once in awhile I'd go to the front to collect large drop offs or something like that. Every once in awhile one of the owners would come in. Either a white guy or a big white guy. The big guy didn't smile and some days he would acknowledge me other days he wouldn't. We never knew when they were coming and they'd look over the books and hang around a little. The other guy would talk to some of the customers. He was a likeable man. I was going to take my lunch when a deep voice caught my attention. I rounded the corner and Malcolm was standing there looking at me like he knew I was coming around the corner. Immediately I thought of Whispers and how the three of them have bonded and how Eugene is probably pissed off somewhere vowing to knock me out the moment he saw me. For the first time ever I looked at my son. He was tall and solid just like his daddy and grandfather. His clothes were nice but not flashy. His jeans were crisp and fresh like he pressed them, not a wrinkle on him. Although his complexion mirrors Whispers, he does look more like Eugene than Whispers. I silently hoped I'd get to see him and Whispers together. It just seemed like they would be mirror images. Malcolm told me to come with him. I followed him out the door. He asked me where I was going to go eat. I shrugged and said I was probably going to get a couple tacos for a dollar; I didn't have a lot of time. He told me to get in the car. I was confused; last I knew this was my Momma's car. I smiled internally when the thought occurred that maybe he came to tell me my momma died. He took me through a drive in, he ordered for me then he gave me my food. I asked him why he didn't get anything and he shrugged. He drove down to the docks. He told me to come on. I looked around at the trucks coming and going. The men who were all busy at work. I followed Malcolm inside the warehouse up stairs to a room with a table. My nephews were sitting at the table in the middle of the floor and there were men all over this room. Some were white, Latin, you name it. No one was smiling and they stopped talking when I walked in the room. "This is Pam, Pam this is everyone." Then Malcolm told me to sit.

I started getting nervous, I was beyond late. Troy looked at me, "Malcolm didn't tell you that you weren't going back?"

"No."

"Pam, you're not going back today." He called out without looking at me. Then he went back to what he was saying to the group.

It made no sense for me to be here, I didn't know what they were talking about. I quietly sat over to the side waiting to understand. Then he walked in the room as a lot of the guys left. Eugene was still fine! His eyes swept the room and he looked right past me without recognition. Malcolm watched me for a reaction to Eugene, but I couldn't pull it back. An older white man approached me, "Pam is it?" I shook my head yes. He held my hands and led me to the table next to him. All of my nephews watched me, Eugene wasn't paying attention. "Thank you for coming down here today. Did Malcolm tell you why we asked to speak with you?" I shook my head no. "Of all of Barb's immediate children you seem to be the only one who left and hasn't returned." Eugene looked at me; it felt like the heat was turned on in this room. "Your son and nephews are divided on sympathy for this old woman. I'm looking for an outside opinion of her."

"What do you mean?"

"Would you plead for her life?" He asked me point blank.

I opened my mouth but nothing came out. I couldn't form a complete thought. I wanted to say no, Heck No!

Nothing was coming out. We're talking about my momma. I kept trying to talk but I couldn't say anything. "Come on Pam!" Fuzzy pleaded. "She's gotten worse without Macio. It's like she don't care about nobody no more. The closest she comes to caring about anyone is Malcolm."

"We all know how much she loves me!" Malcolm said sarcastically.

"What happened?"

"She came to my parent's house claiming you were in the hospital. Almost got herself killed."

"Your parents?" I glanced at Eugene.

Malcolm watched my eyes. "Yes. Oh yeah. I have a son." He said that like it was nothing.

"She don't need the money! Why does she treat us like all we are to her is money?" Fuzzy was angry.

"She grew up without money, she went hungry a lot before. She had a brother Leonard who died right after she met my daddy. He was the only family she had, her parents were killed. Having Macio brought our daddy back. That was how she held on to him. The more kids she had the more difficult it became for daddy to deny my momma to his then wife. Meanwhile she was running behind the scenes helping his business along and throwing caution to the wind. My daddy was her entire world and her pregnancy with Macio was probably her only child born from love. The rest of us are here as part of her survival. My daddy was older when they got together, she had to make sure she was going to be taken care of."

"How do you know all this?" Fuzzy asked.

"Macio used to tell me all kinds of stuff about our parents."

"That explains your messed up name." Troy laughed at Leonard.

Leonard was not amused, "opposed to Troy?"

"Your father was into Greek Mythology. Both of your parents are bookworms. You were named after a land that has been discussed and debated over the years. Be proud of your name and wear it with pride." Eugene said to Troy.

All four boys stared at Eugene. "Stop it with these games. Either you're going to tell me where my father is or you stop talking." Troy said.

"Eugene knows where a lot of people's father's are." I stared at him.

"Pam? You know him?" Malcolm asked like he knew the answer.

"Anyways, so Momma Shuga gets a pass for now?" Eugene said putting the meeting back on track.

The older man shook his head at Eugene. "One day you're going to regret this." Then he looked at me, "thank you for coming down today. Don't worry about your job. They were informed that you would be back business as usual tomorrow." Then I walked out holding on to Pops' arm. Eugene stared hard at me. I got in the car with Malcolm but he didn't start the engine. He pulled his wallet out and took out a picture of a little caramel colored boy. I gasped as I looked at him. He said he calls him Drew. I found myself wanting to hug this little boy. That immediately made me feel bad cause I never allowed myself to feel anything like that towards Malcolm. I thanked Malcolm for sharing. He looked at me, and then he asked me if I knew Whispers. I didn't understand the question. I thought Whispers was going to tell him everything. However it didn't seem like they knew too much. I nodded my head yes, he exhaled and then he said Whispers died a few years ago while I was in jail. I exploded into tears. I couldn't even pull it back. Malcolm watched me cry for a long time. I looked at my watch; Archie was waiting for me at my job. I told Malcolm I had to go. He stood up and asked Troy if he was coming or not. Eugene watched as Troy slid in the car with us and we drove off. Troy asked why I was crying. He said he told me about Whispers. Then he looked at me, he asked me point blank if Whispers was his father. I said no although I wished he was. Malcolm stared at me then he drove on. "Troy, how's your momma doing?"

"She has her good days."

"Good days? Is she ok?"

"I've restricted her from the house, Momma Shuga always messes with her. Pushes her too far!"

"You've restricted your momma?" I turned to look at him.

"I take care of her just like she's always taken care of me."

I smiled at Malcolm, "guess that means you should start beating on me."

"At least you know." Malcolm did not smile.

"What is your son like? Does he act like you? His momma?"

"Too soon to know. He watches me though."

"That's all you ever did was watch people and as soon as you learned to read you put your nose in a book." Then I looked at Troy, "you got any babies?"

"A little girl." He smiled proudly.

"I bet your momma loves that!" I smiled.

"When she gets to see her. Her momma's a trip."

Carey Anderson

"Yeah but it's never as bad as Jason got." Malcolm mentioned.

"Jason?"

"The guy who saved your life the day I wasn't in the mood for you. Leonard's best friend."

"What happened to him?"

Troy explained that Jason was with Leonard's girlfriend's best friend. She pops up pregnant and Jason pops the question. Leonard's girl blows the whistle on Jason's girl. She tells them that Jason's girl is cheating on him and she doesn't think the baby is his. Jason's so in love that he chooses to believe his girl. The baby clearly is not Jason's but she still lying. Jason came home off script and caught her and her baby daddy in the act. Jason killed the guy and has been locked up since. I asked Troy if he was sure his daughter was his. He said she looks just like his momma and he had her tested.

We pulled up to the cleaners and Troy started laughing. He said he couldn't believe I was still with Archie. We all got out of the car and Archie did not look happy. "What's going on?" He put his hands out.

Malcolm extended his hand to shake Archie's hand. "I literally kidnapped her, it wasn't her fault and I didn't give her a choice."

"Why?"

"As you know, my grandma's a little twisted. My cousins and I are divided on the issue of her. I made her come as the voice of reason. Pam has just as many reasons as the rest of us to hate her, but she still has a soft spot for her."

"Did you violate your probation?" Archie asked me.

"All she did was sit in a warehouse with business men. I'm never the reason she gets in trouble."

Archie looked at Malcolm from eye to eye like he was searching for something. Malcolm stood there waiting. "I know you love your momma son, I'm trying to help her get better for you."

Troy started laughing and Malcolm's body jerked. "You ain't told him the story of me and you?" I didn't say anything. "She don't love me and I respond in kind. You two have a good evening." Malcolm and Troy got back in the car.

I started crying all over again and I buried my head in Archie's chest. I told him about Whispers, I even admitted I was disappointed that he didn't do the dirty work for me. Archie let me get it all out.

In the morning he dropped me off to work as usual. When Theresa and I walked inside Eugene was standing there. He apologized for scaring us as I put my knife that Theresa didn't know I carried away. Eugene looked at me with sad eyes then he said his father died. I told him Malcolm told me yesterday. He asked me to come with him and I refused. He followed me to the back begging me. Theresa told us to go out back when our voices carried. I told Eugene that I couldn't believe he thought that I would go anywhere after the way he's treated me, my son, and Leonard. I told him he always tried to treat me like a hooker and like my feelings didn't matter but who was begging who right now. Then I got in his face, I told him I heard him every time he told me he loved me. I felt it every time he kissed my stomach and rubbed it. I told him he asked me to move and then he left me when I was completely vulnerable with the child he made me have! Eugene grabbed my face and kissed me. I tried to fight it at first but this was the kiss my heart aches for. Our kiss was escalating when I backed away from him. I cursed him again then I went to work.

****

Archie was too excited. His job was sending him to Arizona for training for his new promotion. He was going to be gone for a week. He was nervous about being away from me that long. He said he was going to call from the hotel using his calling card as soon as he got there. Since I didn't have a driver's license I was going to take the bus to and from work. We went grocery shopping to make sure I had everything I needed then Archie left Sunday night for the airport. I didn't sleep well without him; the house seemed like it made noises that I never noticed before. Archie called me when he got to his room. We talked until I fell asleep to the sound of his voice.

In the morning I got up. Made breakfast, did my morning exercise. Showered then I just made my bus. I gave myself a hard time for thinking of Eugene. I actually had a pretty normal day, until quitting time. Eugene was waiting for me, I didn't know how to react. I stood there frozen staring at Eugene. I told him my boyfriend was going to be here any minute and he needed to leave. Eugene shook his head at me then he told me I'm always lying. Then he told me to get in his car. I shook my head no and I repeated myself. Eugene walked up to me and gently hugged me. He whispered *PLEASE*! In my ear like it was killing him to hear me tell him no. I felt myself melt as I let him lead me into his car. He politely asked me if I was hungry. I shrugged; I had a pep talk with myself. He wants me to show that I care so he can tell me how much he doesn't care. He'll be cruel and throw money at me or something. Archie wouldn't get back to the hotel until after dinner with his coworkers so I had some time. The host showed us to a two-sided booth. I expected Eugene to sit across from me but he told me to scoot over. Then he sat next to me; the waiter asked if he could bring us something to drink. Eugene asked for a bottle of something and I called out for water. I started to open the menu and Eugene took it from me and then he told me he was ordering

154

for us. He stared at me like he was taking me in while I stared at my empty hands. Eugene said I've lost weight and I nodded, I lost a few inches not so much weight. The doctor said that all those drugs messed up my body and that I would always carry some weight but I still needed to try to be as healthy as possible. Sometimes my hands shake for a few minutes then they stop. Eugene exhaled and then he said he arranged Archie's promotion. I looked at him trying to see if he was lying. But I didn't tell him Archie's name, and I was saying he was coming how would he know unless it were true. I asked why he did it. He said he was happy that someone was looking after me. He wanted to know why I didn't jump on the opportunity to get rid of my momma. I slumped and said I couldn't do it. It was like someone put the gun in my hand and I couldn't pull the trigger. I asked him how Whispers died. Eugene ran his hand over his face and he exhaled. He said that Whispers called him after he saw me, and then they argued cause Whispers told him he already set up a meeting with Malcolm and Leonard. He said he was so angry cause his father was about to expose him. He said his father was so focused on Malcolm and Leonard he wasn't watching his back like he should've. Before he could tell the boys they were ambushed. Then when they thought they had it all under control Whispers got shot. He said Whispers didn't tell them anything more than he and Malcolm had the same name. His breathing was heavy; he said if he would've been there everything would be different. I asked him what is so bad about the boys knowing now? He doesn't see Belle anymore. He said too much time has passed and now they work for his boss. He said it's hard to come clean after all this time. I shook my head cause I understood. To lighten the mood I told him about when Archie introduced himself as Malcolm's possible father. Eugene erupted into laughter just like my nephews did. I asked him why that was so funny. He asked how Malcolm could be Malcolm if Archie was his father. He said that put a whole lot of pressure on my family genes to create my little mastermind. I watched his face, "we have a grandson."

Eugene stopped laughing. "I've seen Malcolm's son."

"And?"

"You seen one bastard you've seen them all." He tried to act like he didn't care. "He got his head so far up that little girl's butt. I don't care if she is the bosses daughter." Then irritation was all over him. "You should see the way he is with them. They got him all in the family. They... They...." Eugene was mad as he looked for the words. "They're brain washing him, making him soft."

"How?"

"I don't know, dangling that girl in his face. Her father took him under his wing and they're together a lot." Jealousy was all over him. "Her mother is even in on the act."

"What her mother do?"

"He does stuff for her all the time. She acts like she's his momma."

"What?" I didn't know why I was jealous, I never wanted him. "That's only as long as he's good to their daughter."

"I guess, but they aren't..." He caught himself. He smiled at me. "Are we honestly sitting here jealous over a kid neither one of us ever wanted?"

"Are you finally admitting that Malcolm is your son?"

"No, I can't."

I rolled my eyes and looked away. I gave him one-word answers the rest of dinner. When he tried to kiss me I turned my head. I got out of the car and ran inside. I locked the door and then I got in the shower. I talked to Archie who was so excited about his new position.

The next day was the same thing, Eugene took me out to dinner then I ran in the house. Wednesday night we were sitting at our table and I felt myself kind of giving in to the idea. I looked up and Malcolm was walking towards our table and a girl was following him. I quickly asked Eugene if that was the mother and he said no. Malcolm looked from Eugene to me like he was trying to put something together. He told the girl to sit at the table next to us. "Eugene, Pam." He said as he sat down.

"Malcolm," we said in unison.

"What is this?"

"I was about to ask you the same."

Malcolm looked from me to Eugene. "Since when you two hang out?"

"That don't look like the bosses daughter."

"Malcolm I'd like to meet the baby."

"Why? You want to beat on him too? Or maybe you'll be nice to him cause he's lighter than me. As much as I can control it you will never see my children."

"Children? You have more?"

"Not yet, soon though."

"Instead of day dreaming about that girl you need to be paying attention."

Malcolm looked at Eugene, "does sitting next to her make you feel it's ok to take an authoritative tone with me? You've had your opportunity to speak; my life is none of your business. I suggest you watch your back with that one and worry about your own life." Then he looked at me. "You need to go home, your man doesn't deserve this. He don't care about anyone but himself."

"Hold on young buck, you can't come over here all in our business."

Malcolm looked from Eugene to me. "You two have something you want to tell me?"

"Yea, she's pregnant and its triplet girls! Surprise you're gonna be a big brother." Eugene was irritated, "what kind of dumb question is that?"

"You need to calm down, you look so guilty." Malcolm said.

Eugene got even more angry, "cause you came over here ruining my good vibes. What if I told her about your kid you're abandoning to be here right now?" He pointed at the girl.

"My son is not a secret, anyone who needs to know about him does. I would never abandon my child like animals do in the wild. I maybe savage on some things, but my family is not one of them." Then he looked at me, "except you of course." Then he stood up and got our waiter's attention. "I'll pay for their meal."

"Why would you do that?" Eugene spit.

Malcolm looked at Eugene, "to mess with your head of course. It's suddenly clear that you need to talk to me about something. You know where to find me when you man up."

Eugene shot out of his seat; "I don't need to talk to you about anything!"

"You're Whispers' son aren't you? Or would you deny your father as well?" Eugene stood there getting madder and madder. "You two have a good evening." Then he told the girl to come on.

On the way home I told Eugene he should just tell Malcolm.

Eugene was too angry to think about what I was saying. I could see him shutting down in front of me. Then he told me I needed to invite him in. So much for the nice guy I've spent the last few days with. When he held up money and told me he knew I was worth it, I got out of the car and slammed my front door shut.

****

"Pam can you come?" Theresa called out as she went back to her customer.

The nice owner was here and he was out front talking to the customer as well. It was that woman AGAIN! She had a baby on her hip and she was smiling. The baby was laughing really hard at the owner who was being really silly. I wasn't going to pay the baby any attention until I got close and realized it was Malcolm's son. I felt frozen as I tried to get it together. In person looking at that baby I knew he was Malcolm's son. The woman stopped smiling as she looked at me. She looked at the baby then me. "Dito? Who's this?"

"This is Pam, she's a whiz on the permanent press."

"Pam this is my Auntie Annette."

"Hi," then I pointed to the baby. "He's really cute, how old is he?"

"Thank you he's almost three." She watched my eyes. "I've seen you before haven't I?" I shrugged, "well I doubt you know my daughter. You know his father or something?"

The baby looked at me with Whispers' squint. I lost it and ran out the back. Every time I see that woman she has something I want. She's the one who plays momma to my son! Malcolm probably gets happy to see her. Hearing the door open snatched me from my thoughts. The woman came out; all kindness was gone from her eyes. I wiped my tears and straightened up, she probably came out here to gloat. Who knows what Malcolm's told her about me. She stopped just outside of my reach and looked at me. "You're Malcolm's momma." I could hear her breathing. I balled my fist and looked at her in her eyes. "I've heard a little about you, it's nice to put my eyes on you." She looked me up and down. "Why are you crying?"

"That's my grandson."

She exhaled, "it looks like our children are back together. Maybe they'll come by so you can meet."

I shook my head no, "if you've heard about me you know that's not going to happen."

She stared at me, "if you try anything I will break your neck!" Her eyes were cold. "Come on." When we walked back inside Theresa was at the register with big eyes watching everything. Annette picked up the little boy and then she brought him close. "Say hi to Andrew."

My chest started aching, "hi Andrew."

"Hi." He said softly.

"He's beautiful!"

Annette stared at me, "just like his daddy."

"Yes," I put my hands out to him. "Can I hold him?"

She looked at Andrew who was looking me over. "If he wants you to." Then she looked down at him.

I held my hands out to him, he looked at my hands and then he laid his head on her shoulder. His way of rejecting me. I guess this is payback for everything I've done to Malcolm. I rubbed his back; at least I knew he was real and not a figment of my imagination.

****

Archie's oldest was telling us about the fight she had at school today. I was twirling my spaghetti listening to the way this little girl puts her spin on the details. She has a gift for story telling. "Pam?" A woman's voice called me from the story.

I looked up and it was Melanie. Her hair was completely grey and long. "Melanie!" I stood up and hugged her. "Archie it's my sister."

"Hello," she said with sad eyes.

"These are his girls, how are you?" I smiled.

"You didn't hear?" She searched my eyes. "Malcolm's in jail."

I sat down and held my breath, "for?"

"Murder, and a bunch of other charges." Immediately tears poured out of her eyes. "Leonard died!"

I popped up and hugged her. "NO!"

"Malcolm saw that they got him and he thought the people who got Leonard had his son and girlfriend. The trial is in a couple weeks." She cried.

"Why didn't anyone tell me about the funeral?"

"Funeral? The only funerals momma paid for was daddy and Macio's."

"What about his father?"

"Belle completely lost it and we didn't see her for a long time. Now she's just staying high."

"What about her other kids?"

"Leonard was her first born. His girlfriend was pregnant but she lost the baby behind the stress. Momma acts like she doesn't care. I personally think she had something to do with it." Melanie put her hand over her mouth. "Fuzzy and Troy have been losing it. This is all too much Pam!"

I wrote my number down, "please call me and let me know when the court date is. I want to go."

"I'm sorry for interrupting your meal. I never see you." She looked at the number, "I'm going to call you as soon as I know."

Archie was mad the rest of the dinner. The girls had so many questions; they didn't know I had a son. They waited for me to answer in between sobs. If I would've known the last time I saw Leonard was going to be the last time I saw him I would've hugged him. Told him I loved him. Something! When we got in the car urgency came over me. "Can you take me to Fuzzy's?"

"No!"

"No?"

"No! I have my daughters in the car. Your family don't mean you know good. You can't go and get sucked right back in by them!"

"Archer! My nephew is dead! This is outside of the box!"

"No!"

"You don't own me! Pull over! I will find my own way there!"

"Pam! Let's just go home."

"How can you be so heartless with my family, but your grandmother gets the sniffles and we gotta fly up to Santa Rosa and stare at her blowing her nose? You're taking off work, pulling the girls out of school like its life or death. Pull over!"

"Pam! If I pull this car over and you get out, I'm throwing all of your stuff away! You can come get it out the trash!"

Fire burned in my throat! "MY NEPHEW IS DEAD! MY SON IS IN JAIL! AND YOU'RE WORRIED ABOUT THE CONTROL YOU HAVE OVER ME! PULL OVER!" I screamed as I opened my door.

The girls screamed to their father to let me out. As soon as I got out of the car I saw the bus coming in the opposite direction. I ran across the busy street and I got on the bus. I sat down crying an angry. I wasn't going to my momma's house; I'm going to Fuzzy's place. I sunk in my seat, what if he moved? I hadn't thought of that.

When I knocked on the door, someone snatched it open immediately. I didn't recognize this guy at all. "What?" He was impatient.

"Does Fuzzy live here?"

"Who are you?" He looked me up and down.

"Pam."

"Melanie somebody named Pam is at the door looking for Fuzzy."

Melanie hurried out of the bedroom and she rushed to me. She told me to come in and then she hugged me while we cried. "Pam, this is my husband Ernest."

"Husband?"

"Yes, this is Troy's daddy." She tried to smile.

I looked at him, I didn't see it. Troy look so much like Melanie I guess it wasn't meant to be seen. "Hello."

"Where's your man?"

"We got in a fight. He didn't want me to come. It's not like I went to momma's house."

"I don't go over there. I stay away from her as much as I can."

Melanie told me as much as she could about everything that happened. She called Fuzzy, and then he and Troy came over. Fuzzy broke down with me; I told him I didn't wish evilness on Belle. They said she's cracked out somewhere and to let her go. Troy kept looking at his daddy like he didn't like him or something. I imagined Troy being happy about knowing his father finally after all this time. Fuzzy volunteered to take me home, and he said if Archie was serious about putting me out then I could come stay at his place. "Troy your father seems nice."

Troy blew air, "that's not my dad. That's her husband, but that's not my father."

"Why would she say he was if he wasn't?"

"Cause that's the guy she married, that's not the man who fathered me. I met him when all this blew up."

"Wait a minute, Melanie was with more than one person?"

Troy got irritated, "Auntie it's too much going on right now. I can't even go into all of that. That's my momma's husband, but he's not my father or daddy or anything like that."

"You have his last name?"

"Technicality, just like anything else." Troy was over this conversation.

When we pulled up to Archie's house he was outside pacing. He had his keys in his hand like he wanted to go, but he didn't know where to go. He sighed out loud when I got out of the car. He hurried to me and apologized. He thanked Fuzzy and Troy for bringing me home. Then he invited them in. He said the girls gave him such a hard time as soon as I got out of the car. They told him he was wrong and they were proud of me for sticking up for myself. It bothered me that he didn't get it when I said it, but I was happy to know the girls had my back. I hugged both of them so tight and thanked them. Troy looked surprised when he saw me hugging the girls. He probably thought I was incapable of hugs. Troy told Fuzzy it was time to go.

****

"Glad you could make it." Annette said as she stood next to me. I didn't know where she came from, but I was relieved to see her. "That's the mother." She pointed to a woman who looked more hard in the face than me. Annette pointed out all of the victim's family as they filled in the courtroom. We sat in the corner in the back watching everyone come in. All of the victim's family sat together in a few rows, and then they looked around at everybody in the courtroom. When they brought Malcolm in his eyes swept the room. His brows moved when he saw me sitting next to Annette. Annette had a pencil and paper and she took notes as each of those girls got up their talking about their love for my son. Not one of these girls or women were the same. The only thing they had in common was brown skin. They ranged from a light cocoa brown to deep chocolate browns. At lunchtime Annette told me to let everyone walk out first and then she told me to follow her as we went in the opposite direction of everyone. She reached in her purse and she gave me a sandwich and an apple. It was like she knew I was coming or something. She didn't make chitchat or anything. She looked around at the people who came near us and she ate. We were the first to go back to our seats. My son had a long list of females who thought he was so special. I wondered if they were giving him what he felt he needed from me. I asked

Annette if any of these girls was her child and she said no. When it was time to go, Annette didn't say anything she just got up and left. The following morning Annette appeared out of nowhere again. We sat in the corner an then a white girl went on the stand. When the lawyer kept trying to make her angry, I looked at Annette. Annette was gripping her pencil and shaking her leg like that was the only thing holding her back. I stared at that little girl and then I looked at Annette. When she frowned at the lawyer that's when I saw the resemblance that was her baby. I touched Annette's hand and she took a deep breath. Her daughter did well. They tried to make her fall apart and she didn't say anything against my son. When I saw Rita go up on the stage and then her father I was relieved that they were on our side.

When we came back for sentencing, the victim's family was upset. Annette wrote everything down, she told me congratulations, and then she left.

****

"I remember you from school. You were always quiet and reading books." Archie told Melanie.

"Guilty, sometimes… Who am I kidding? Most times I needed to escape the reality of my family. I'd get lost in a book and that saved me."

"I don't remember you reading books." I was jealous and I don't know why.

"Cause I couldn't really read at home. Momma would get mad if she saw me reading. The only reason she let Malcolm get away with it is because Macio told her it was good for him. And you know Macio could talk her into most things."

"How did you meet Ernest?" I didn't want to talk about Malcolm.

"Field trip," she smiled.

"I never seen someone so beautiful in my life." Then he kissed her.

"You don't seem like someone who would be friends with Eugene."

"Eugene?" Ernest asked.

Melanie's smile dropped, "Leonard's father."

"Oh," Ernest sucked his teeth. "She don't know the story of us?" Melanie shook her head no. "I met her first, I loved her first. I was in there first, your evil sister talked her into double dating with her and that's when she met him." He moved his hands around angry. "All that happened and I come back to rescue my wife and she's pregnant before we can be together again." He drummed his fingers, "I walked away. It's still hard to look at him."

"It's not Troy's fault."

"I know, but we got a understanding, he stay out of my way and I stay out of his."

"They do that don't they, you turn your back for a minute and they having the next man's baby." Archie said shaking Ernest's hand.

I rolled my eyes at Melanie who was looking sad. "Boo who! Cause while we were out getting our workout, you can't lie to us and say you were sitting at home mending your broken hearts. This one married someone else and tried to think he could have a family with anyone other than me."

Ernest started laughing, "true but I needed to get my head right." He touched Melanie's hand. I had Melanie laughing so much; her man kept looking at her and smiling. "Pam you are alright! I was leery of doing anything with any of her family members. All your brothers and sisters, well you know your family. You are the only decent one in that whole family."

"And yet I'm a liar and a thief." Archie touched my hand at my failed attempt to poke fun at myself.

Melanie grabbed my hands. "We all got something we battle with. You've always been good to me. Your son is just like my own."

I wiped my eyes, "Malcolm?"

"He's a wonderful young man. I've written him letters once a month since he went in. He sends thank you's through Troy. I think his spirits are low. Have you thought about going to see him?"

"For what? I'd rather find my grandson."

Melanie gave me a disappointed smile. "I know it's easier when it doesn't directly come from you but...."

I cut her off, "what do you mean?"

Melanie cleared her throat then she locked her eyes on me. "Malcolm is your son! You love him, but you don't know how to be good to him. You were never hugged or treated good so it's hard to give it to the reflection of you. Stop trying to act like you don't care. You love Malcolm, you just don't know how to show it."

"I don't care about him!"

"So it doesn't bother you that he calls his in-laws momma and dad?"

I got so angry! "He actually calls them that? I know he thinks of them that way, but! But! BUT! THAT'S TOO FAR! IS THAT WHY THAT LADY DID ALL THAT CAUSE SHE KNOWS THAT'S WRONG?" Everybody watched me. "He's nice to her isn't he? He hugs her? He look at her like she can save him don't he?"

"He loves her very much."

"What about me?"

"Go tell him you care. He needs to know."

****

Archie and I argued for a long time about it. He wasn't against me going to see Malcolm, once I understood that I calmed down a lot. His thing was that he didn't want me showing that my motivation in coming to see him was that for once I felt the affects of someone stealing from me. I watched Malcolm talk to Archie. Malcolm even smiled at Archie, which is something he rarely does. Archie said he was going to tell him how he's always thought of Malcolm like a warrior. Then he was going to say any other thing he thought would encourage him.

When I sat down Malcolm watched my eyes. All the words I thought I was going to say flew out of my mind. "You've been hanging out with Aunt Melanie."

"Yes, Archie and Ernest get a long pretty well."

"How did Aunt Melanie get you to come here?"

"Get me to come?"

"You want me to believe that you came here out of concern like a mother would? Get real! I know you're not here for money, so put it out there."

"Annette."

"My momma, what about her?"

169

I couldn't believe he said that to me so matter of factly like it was second nature to him. "Your momma?"

He narrowed his eyes at me. "Pam! You may have given birth to me, but you don't have a maternal bone in your body."

"I'm here!"

"You're here out of jealousy, spite, possession. Not for the reason you should be here. You don't love me, you never have."

"I'm your mother of course I do."

"Name one thing you've done for me."

"I gave birth to you!"

He squinted his eyes, "really? You kind of had to once you realized I was there. Whether you wanted to or not you had to do that. Can you name anything else?" I lowered my head as I tried to think. "I know what you could do. Tell me what I already know. Tell me who my father is."

"Why is she special enough for you to call her momma?"

"She loves me!"

"Because you're with her daughter."

"I'm not with her daughter. She comes to see me regularly, sometimes just to look at me and build me up. She loves me!"

"Probably cause you give her money."

"That woman is a millionaire, she doesn't need my pennies. I was like you when I met her. My momma has shown me love, discipline, and kindness. All of it comes from her heart. She don't want or need anything from me, but my love as a son in return.

Real love is such a foreign concept to you that you try to ruin it for everyone else. Pam, that man don't love you and he never will. Why do you protect him?"

I shook my head, "I can't believe I fell for this! Your ugly monkey behind don't know nothing about nothing. That woman doesn't love you! She's using you! She's playing up nice to you for her daughter's sake. You the stupid idiot who's falling for it. That little boy is too light to be your son! That's not even your baby!" I was lying; I knew that was his son. He hurt me with his words.

"Now you sound like your momma. Sell crazy somewhere else, I ain't buying. You know that is my son! I know that Drew is my son! My momma don't need me for anything. She chooses to love me because she's a beautiful and loving person. A concept you know nothing about. Don't come back here Pam! Leave me alone! Leave my family alone! If I feel like you've even thought about my family I'm putting you down!"

"You're threatening me?"

"It's not a threat, it's a promise!" Then he stood up and walked away.

Chapter 9

"You said you didn't know who the girl was."

"HUH?"

"You said your momma said she stole from her and you didn't know who she was. Now you just said you saw her in the court room."

"I didn't recognize her at first. You know how much happened in my life between the time I saw her and today? I didn't immediately know who she was."

"You knew! Just like you knew who Drew was as soon as you saw him."

I put my hand over my mouth. I was about to blow. The unfriendly guy gave me a paper bag just in time. My stomach emptied everything into it. The room spun and I broke out in a sweat. He chirped, "she just threw up and her pupils are dilated."

"I'm almost there!"

He looked at me, "can you talk?"

I took a look around the room everything was blurred. "Yes, I'm not finished."

He frowned, "you are so stubborn."

"I gotta finish, please!" Then I threw up a little more. I used my shirt to wipe my mouth. I told myself I could do this.

~

Archie and I were at Melanie's. We were waiting for Ernest to come home so we could go out to eat. Archie left to go meet Ernest at the bus stop. Melanie and I told him to hurry cause we were hungry and they could talk about us later. Troy bought Melanie a new car, but he told her not to let Ernest drive it. Ernest was mad about it, but Troy said he didn't trust Ernest. We heard gunshots screeching tires and then a few minutes later another pop. Melanie jumped really hard then she froze in place. We were looking around but no one moved. Suddenly there was frantic knocking on the door and sounds of little kids screaming and crying. Melanie ran to the door. Most of the kids were hysterical. "Auntie Melanie! Auntie Melanie! It's Sterling! Help! Help!" They screamed.

Melanie screamed then she took off running and all the kids ran behind her screaming and crying. I ran behind them. My nephew was on the ground struggling. Melanie started trying to do CPR on him. She screamed to them to call 911! I asked where my momma was. They said she left just before this happened. The police and paramedics came fast. I didn't exactly pay attention to the police car that sped around the corner and the second ambulance that went behind it. The paramedics started working on little Sterling and then they took him to the hospital, Melanie got in the ambulance. The police talked to everyone, the neighbors, and the kids. They took pictures of all the bullet holes on the house. The tire marks on the ground, everything. Tiffany was screaming she said she already knew her little brother was gone. All the kids stood around hugging each other. Momma would've never allowed us to comfort each other before. Renee came down the street with her little ones in a stroller and a couple walking. She hurried then she asked what happened. Then she asked where Sterling was. Everyone kept crying and she fell to the ground screaming. Troy and Fuzzy pulled up looking completely angry. Fuzzy asked who got hit, the kids cried as they said Sterling. Fuzzy bent over to grab air as Troy cursed. Then Troy looked at me and asked where his momma was. I told him she went to the hospital with Sterling. Then he asked where Ernest and my shadow were. I forgot all about Archie. I ran back towards Melanie's apartment. When I got to the corner I saw the police cars at the end of the block. I ran back to Melanie's place and Archie wasn't inside. My heart sank as I ran back out and towards the crowd of people. Ernest was in handcuffs and I didn't see Archie. I yelled out to Ernest asking him where Archie was. His eyes were evil as he looked at me and he didn't respond. One officer asked who I was to Archer Rudd, and I told him I was his wife. It's not like they could make me prove it on the spot. The officer said he was taken to the hospital cause he was shot in a drive by shooting. I asked them why they cuffed Ernest and no one would answer me. Fuzzy came over and I told him everything. Fuzzy made his hand like a gun and he pointed at Ernest. Then the police took Ernest away. Troy was looking out the window and Fuzzy didn't utter a peep. When we got to the hospital we went to the emergency room. You could hear Melanie crying all the way out in the lobby. Troy walked past everyone and hurried to his momma. He put his arms around her as she cried into his chest. I asked the nurse where Archie was and I hurried to him with Fuzzy on my heels. The doctor was explaining that the bullet passed through his stomach, and he was going to need surgery. When the doctor walked out Fuzzy walked up on Archie. "You better hope that I find that you're clean!"

"Why wouldn't he be clean? What's going on?" I looked between them.

"I told Ernest to call it off. I told him she wasn't there."

I sat down in the chair. "You were trying to kill my momma?"

"No, but I knew Ernest was going to."

"How do you know?"

"Back in the day I used to put in work for Ernest. I don't live like that no more. Everything that's happened with your son has ripples that trickle down baby. That kid he killed has a big family."

"HAD!" Fuzzy barked.

"Had." Archie swallowed. "Your momma is on they side."

"Against Malcolm?"

"Yes, she's stepping on everybody's toes trying to make allies because she don't have them no more. Ernest said she had to go."

"We are the only ones who say when she goes down. My little cousin, a little kid! He was killed over something he don't even know about. Ernest is dead, now you can tell me who pulled the trigger or take their place."

"Fuzzy?"

"NAW Auntie! Stay out of this!"

Archie exhaled, "Ernest. I saw him get out the car a block away and he shot me when he knew I knew."

Troy walked in the area, "so then my momma's gonna be a widow."

"I'll let Malcolm know he's coming." Fuzzy said.

****

I started going over Melanie's house as much as I could. Troy said he was going to buy a place for her cause he didn't want her so close to my momma's house anymore. He bought her a little house far enough, but not too far away. I was walking from the bus stop to Melanie's to help her pack when a car pulled up next to me. "Pam!" It was my momma. She has been trying to get in contact with me. I keep seeing random nieces and nephews all over the place.

"Momma?"

"Baby I'm so happy I saw you. I need your help. Acacia is going shopping for me, I need you to help her."

"HUH?"

"Don't HUH me! You see all those kids I got in that house. I need help getting everything. Get in the car!"

"Momma I'm tired. I just got off work and...."

"Pam! Get in this car RIGHT NOW!"

I felt like a child as I got in the backseat.

"You got everything you need?" She asked Acacia.

"Yes."

"Acacia how's your daddy I haven't seen him in a long time."

"He alright I guess, he stay with his crack head girlfriend."

"Oh."

"Acacia go in here exactly like I told you and everything will be fine."

"Grandma," she whined.

My momma hit her a couple times. "Stop all this whining! Who's been taking care of you since you was little? When your no good daddy ran away and your momma came up missing? Get in there like I told you! I'm gonna be right here when you get done."

There was a little voice in the back of my head telling me to get out of the car and run, but I didn't listen. Acacia grabbed a cart and she pushed it inside the store with tears rolling down her face. "Where's your list?"

"I don't got one."

"What are we here for?"

"A couple things." Then she walked ahead. She went to the can food aisle. She threw a bunch of cans in the cart." Then she walked fast ahead of me and got in line. I took a deep breath and then I followed her. "I can do this!" She mumbled to herself.

"Acacia what's going on?"

The checkout girl started ringing up her cans. "Auntie watch my back." Then she took out a gun. She told the girl to put all her money in a bag. The girl accidentally screamed.

"What are you doing?" I asked.

"Get the bag!" Acacia told me.

"No, I didn't come here for this."

Acacia grabbed the bag and ran hard out the door. She got in the car and my momma drove off. The security guard tackled me to the ground and I was charged with armed robbery. Didn't matter that I didn't have a gun or any cash. My record said I was the one. Fortunately the cashier and the customer in line behind me stepped up. They didn't believe that I didn't know Acacia so I had to serve time anyways.

****

"Pam! Your momma means you no good! You have to stay away from her."

"Archie I told you what happened, she caught me off guard."

"So you're done with her?"

"Yes!"

"Good! When you get out we're going to get married."

I smiled, "you're divorced?"

"It's official today!"

I got excited, "you sure you want to marry me?"

"I meant it when I asked you while we were kids."

"I love you!"

"I love you!" He smiled.

That night I thought about Eugene. He's so evil! Archie is always good to me and he doesn't leave me just because I keep ending up in here. This time it truly wasn't my fault.

****

"Momma how could you do that to me?"

She exhaled, "Pam! I'm sorry."

"What?" Her apology caught me off guard. She never apologized before.

"I owe apologies to so many people. Everything is falling apart." She exhaled, how long have you been out?"

"A couple days."

"Let me take you to breakfast."

"My fiancé says I can't talk to you anymore."

"You're talking to me now. You've got to be looking for a job. I can help you; meet me at the restaurant if you're serious about working. I know they're looking for help. I'll put in a good word for you."

"I have a fiancé momma."

"It's a real job, washing dishes I think."

"Meet me in an hour and a half."

"Why so long?"

"I don't drive, got to catch the bus."

"Ok, hurry."

I got dressed and again something told me to stay *hommmme*.

~

My words were slurring. I told myself to focus cause I could do this.

~

When I walked up to the restaurant I took a deep breath. My momma was already sitting and she kept looking at this table across the way. It was two white girls with a definitely black baby at the table. My momma was so mad. I asked her what was wrong. She pointed to one of the girls and said she stole money from her. I looked at the little nothing of a girl and asked how she did that. My momma started talking fast and with her hands. She told me to go over and get her. When I flat out refused she said she was going to tell Archie that we were here if I didn't. I was supposed to snatch that girl up and just beat on her. As I approached her I was trying to figure out why she looked so familiar. I looked at the brown baby's face and I realized he looked like his momma. That's when I realized who she was. I started fussing cause I was here and I had to do something. She cut her eyes at me looking just like her momma. I kept fussing cause I was trying to think of how to get out of this. When the waiter came I went back to the table. I told my momma she was wrong for sending me after my grand son's momma. My momma got mad and started yelling at me asking why I let her go. The girls picked up the baby and hurried out the door. My momma started yelling at me saying I was letting her get away. The waiter came to our table and I headed out the door. Malcolm's words about her momma danced around my mind and I got *mmmmmmm mmmmmm mmmmmad*! *Fuuuuzzzzzyyyyy* was there and he was protecting *hhheerrrr*.

That hurt! I looked at him but there were two of him. "You know what happened, I woke up here."

Then his walkie-talkie chirped, "I'm here!"

Chapter 10

My eyes were getting heavy and sleep was pulling me as I broke out in a sweat. I can finish! I can finish! Then he walked in the door big black and strong. His eyes didn't look at me like the eyes of a man looking at his mother. I could've been road kill for the way he looked at me. He asked how long had it been to the guy. The guy told him he gave me the pills as soon as we got here. He said I've been running my mouth with nervous chatter and I vomited twice. Malcolm cut his eyes at me and asked him if I've said anything else worth knowing. Then the guy said I've been telling my version of my life story. Malcolm looked at me. "Manipulations! Go to sleep Pam!"

"Over a white girl Malcolm?"

"She is the mother of my child! She is the only reason I'm not doing this myself MY WAY! You betrayed me! All your talk about being different when you got out, and the first chance you get you blindly do what Momma Shuga tells you to do! You will follow her to a fault."

"You let the white man tell you who lives and who dies."

"My father didn't want to make the call. He wanted me to spare you. This is my decision."

"Have you lost your mind? He's not your father!"

"Thanks to you, I'll never know who my father is for sure."

"Eugene is your faaaatttthhhheeeer!" I slurred, "Eugene is your daddy."

He looked like he wanted to hit me. "My father is Timothy Wallace! My momma's name is Annette Wallace!"

"Annette?"

"Yes, you've met her. Her daughter is the mother of my son. The girl you tried to fight! Listening to Momma Shuga is the reason why! She got my..." He took a deep breath. "She got Leonard and Sterling killed. She got my uncle killed! Her disease dies with you!" It was getting too hard to keep my eyes open. My head got heavy and it felt like gravity pulled me backwards in my chair.

"But I wasn't going to touch her. Ask Fuzzy, you know me if I was going to get her she *wooooouldve havvvve beeeennnn gooottttenn*!" I couldn't open my eyes. I was fighting but it wasn't working. Malcolm and the unfriendly guy watched me.

~

Slick smiled down at me, "you wiggle like a fish!"

"I heard the rumors and I don't care! I love you Pam!" Archie said embarrassed.

Eugene took my hand and twirled me, "Barb has some beautiful daughters." Then he looked at me with fire in his eyes, "it's not mine!"

"Pam I'm going to ask you again, did you sleep with Eugene? Is this his baby?"

Momma frowned, "what kind of name is Malcolm?"

"You too black to be any good to anybody! I hate you! You're nothing! No one loves you! No one will ever love you!" I screamed in his face.

"She don't love you! You just a nasty little boy!"

"BLACK BOYS DON'T GET TO EAT!"

"Ms. Latour, Malcolm is very special. He's so smart I'd like to place him in advance classes." The principal said.

"He's not special! He's not smart! You're the one who's been feeding his head with all this nonsense! He's too black to ever be anybody important!"

"You embarrass me!" Malcolm turned and walked away.

"Baby, I love you! Please! Come with me! I'll get you help! I love you!"

Belinda screamed, "THEY KILLED MY BABY! THEY KILLED HIM!"

"WHERE'S MALCOLM?"

I opened my eyes one last time as I saw Malcolm walk out the door. He was thanking the guy who put the pills in my hand. I could hear my heartbeat in my ears. My chest felt heavy, I wanted to apologize. I wanted to tell him it was all me, I wanted to take it all back. I inhaled one last time and then everything went black.

****

I was dreaming about Fuzzy when he was little. He looked up at me with those big brown eyes. "Pam!" I looked at him but I couldn't speak. "Pam!" This time he smacked my cheek. I still couldn't speak. "PAM!" This time he slapped me hard! And it hurt! When I opened my eyes Fuzzy's eyes were red and he was about to slap me again.

"I'm dead?" I asked above a whisper, my mouth was completely dry.

Fuzzy looked mean and like he was mad. "Pam do you want to live?"

"Yes!" I moved my tongue around my dry mouth.

"FUZZY! WHAT ARE YOU DOING?" The unfriendly guy yelled.

"Blu! Man, I can't let this happen. I need this one." Fuzzy looked at me with red eyes. "Stay down and don't make a peep. This is the last plea for your life!" I did as I was told. I was laying in the back of a car. I could see trees and a blue sky. I could hear birds, no those are quacks so it has to be ducks, and I can hear water. "Blu, I'm leaving. Malcolm knows I'm gone. I'm gonna take her and he never has to hear from her again. I need you to look away."

"Fuzzy! She's evil! She don't even own up to half the stuff she put Malcolm through. You should've heard the story she told me."

"She also doesn't know half the stuff going on. She just got out; you know Momma Shuga was going to use her as bait. She couldn't stay here without dying anyways. I'm gonna take her, and I'm gonna go."

"Call her out here!" The guy said. "You're on your own if Malcolm finds out. She needs to understand this is serious."

"Pam come out!" I sat up slowly; we were by a pond I didn't know. I scooted to the door and slowly stood myself up next to the car, my head was pounding. I couldn't miss the pile of dirt next to the deep hole that is intended to be my grave. I looked at the shovel and I started crying. The unfriendly guy had a syringe in his gloved hand that I know was intended for me. "Pam! You have to cooperate with me. Your life is at stake here. If you cross me you will die!" I shook my head yes. Fuzzy slowly backed away. "Thank you Blu! Thank you! I'm leaving right now!"

"You're on your own, Malcolm will get you for this."

"I know, I know! I can't let this happen." Fuzzy grabbed my arm then he led me from this unmarked car to a pickup truck. There was a cover over the bed. Fuzzy told me to get in the back and he'd get me out when it was time. As I got in the back of the truck, the unfriendly guy said something real fast into his walkie-talkie. Then I saw him throw the syringe in the hole. I laid down amongst his suitcases and quietly listened. Fuzzy drove for a while and then he stopped the truck when we were on open road. The sun was setting.

"What about Archie? He was going to marry me."

"Obviously that's over. Did he ever tell you what he did all those years when he was away from you?"

"He was making a mess of his marriage."

"Working under Ernest?"

"Right."

"Ernest who is against us?"

"Right."

"Ernest who tried to kill Momma Shuga. Ernest that Jason and Malcolm killed right after they delivered him to their prison."

"Right."

"Ernest who's family told Momma Shuga to bring you to the restaurant so that they could use you against Malcolm. If Momma Shuga wasn't so twisted and evil she should've thought that one through. She had you and Amber, she could've had Malcolm by the balls."

"You're saying Archie still works for them?"

"Catch up Pam, did Archie work for Ernest or did Ernest work for

Archie? Archie always wanted to get to Malcolm."

"But that's because he felt fatherly towards him."

"Maybe in the beginning, but he left you two. He may have asked about him over the years, but once we started becoming strong with the Wallace's didn't he push the issue a little more than usual?"

"Go back a few chapters, Archie wouldn't...."

"Pam! I'm sure that story you were telling was all fluffy. Did you talk about how badly you treated Malcolm? All the reasons why he has every right to put you down?"

"Kind of...."

Fuzzy stepped on the gas. "My momma is dead! DEAD! Because her momma sent her out knowing it would get her killed. She didn't cry or anything when they told her my momma was dead. She mad cause Troy came and said enough was enough and he told her Tiffany and Penny weren't coming back, and if she dared to come to his place she was going to die! You are my only link to kindness before we created it for ourselves. I don't blame Malcolm for wanting you dead. You went against the first person he's ever bonded with! You can't even understand how much Malcolm loves her. You can't even understand all that that little girl has done for our family! We are now a family! The Latour's are strong now, we are no longer divided and it started with her!"

"Fuzzy I wasn't going to hurt her."

"PAM! Don't lie to me! I was there! I know you! You are so jealous about the wrong things. You were going to hurt her because you know he loves her. I don't know what pleasure you get out of hurting Malcolm like you do, but letting you die would hurt me too much. Malcolm thinks you're dead. As far as he's concerned that better never change. You need to change Pam, and if I've got to kick your butt until you do then so be it."

"Malcolm really loves her? What does it feel like to love someone?"

"You've got to let the hate go! All that, that you think you had with Eugene wasn't love. You don't love Archie. This will be your chance to find something real."

"Where are we going?"

"Vegas."

"Why Vegas?"

"Cause you don't know anyone out there. You need to learn to love yourself Pam."

"You love yourself?"

"I'm learning."

"I'm tired of this life anyways."

"This is your clean slate. You get to start over, no more lying. No more stealing! If you cross me Pam I will finish the job Malcolm started."

"Why am I still alive?"

"You vomited. When he determined you were still alive he was going to finish you off."

"My head hurts."

"It should hurt."

"Archie didn't love me?" I didn't want to believe he didn't.

"What difference does love make when business is involved?"

"I told Malcolm about Eugene."

"Malcolm and Leonard discussed that a long time ago. He already knows."

"If he knows why does he ask?"

"To test you, you always fail him."

****

Fuzzy bought a house, and somehow he worked it all out with my probation officer to let me live and work out here. Out here in this HOT dessert sun.

I keep hitting brick walls out here. To be suddenly plucked from anywhere that looks familiar and put in a completely new environment where my nephew is my only companion is hard. After quite a few years I found myself in the middle of a twelve-step program. My sponsor's name is Johnny Mae. At first I wanted to fight her. She kept calling me on my lies and for an ex-junky her memory is pretty intact. I felt like she was judging me when she pushed me. I felt like she thought she was better than me because she had been clean longer. One day I found a picture of me from when I was a lot younger at Fuzzy's. I brought it to my meeting as proof of how beautiful I used to be. When Johnny Mae acted like she wasn't impressed it upset me to the bone. It wasn't until her grandson whom she didn't know she had came to stay with her that she opened up more about her past. He's a handsome kid and he's been through a lot in his short time as an addict. A lot of it sounds like the rich kid whoas to me at first though. He thought his stepmom was his real mom, and then he found out that the woman he hated all his life was his real mother. He made me think about my father who never cared about any of us totally. I mean he cared, but he didn't. My momma never cared, and she made sure we knew it. Then I thought about my own grandson. I wondered how big he is now. Does he even care that they think I'm dead. I wondered if he got any darker like his father, or did he stay his little peanut butter complexion. I can't allow myself to think about Malcolm too much. Thinking about him confuses me. My son wanted me dead, and put someone in charge of making that happen. He turned his back on me. I… I… I'm so sorry for the way things happened, but I would never want a do over. I can't say what would be different if I had it to do all over again. If I saw Eugene right now I'd only want his hands on me. I used to ask Fuzzy about him. If he was married, if he ever talked to Malcolm about what I told him. Was he even bothered a little when they told him I was dead? Fuzzy said he wasn't there for that conversation, and he doesn't talk to Eugene. My memory may be sketchy on a lot of things, but I remember everything about Eugene. The ripples of his muscles, the way he squinted his eyes at me, the sound of his laugh. The noise he made when I completely blew his mind. Then I cry because the only time he was kind of kind to me is when I carried the child he claims he didn't want. The way he protected me then. Yeah, looking back maybe I should've had another baby. Maybe he wanted a little girl. But if she came out like Malcolm he would've ran again. He wasn't going around claiming Leonard, but he didn't flat out deny Leonard like he did Malcolm. I can't say what I would do differently when it comes to Eugene, I guess because when it came to him I did it all. I listened when I didn't want to. I gave in to him in everyway he asked me to. Shoot I had sex with him in Archie and I's bed. Whatever Eugene wanted he got from me, whenever he wanted it. Maybe that was the problem.

My health is a little shaky these days, and the doctors say it's the after affects of all the drugs I used to take. Knowing that I was that close to death has truly opened my eyes. I am the complete opposite of who I used to be. It took me a while to get here though. I had to let the idea of having a man in my life go. I always seem to find the wrong ones and it never works out for me. Instead I got a little dog that I love to pieces and he loves me. I take him everywhere with me. My dog can sense when I'm about to have an episode and I know to get somewhere safe before I spaz out. Some mornings are worse than others and I can't get out of the bed. Sometimes it's not even anything physical; sometimes the stuff running around my head makes it too hard to deal. My doggy gives me someone to love. Fuzzy got married, and has a family of his own. I live in the in-law unit on his property. I've learned to shower Fuzzy's kids with love and attention. It hasn't been easy, but Fuzzy, the only person concerned for my life, has helped me get here. I work for a sightseeing company. Guided tours to and from the Grand Canyon is my normal route, but every once in awhile I work the others. My doggy quietly waits in his carrier for me next to the driver. Sometimes I bring him out, but I mostly keep him hidden. Some people act completely terrified of my little munchkin.

As my guests were getting on the bus I did a double take. My eyes had to be playing a trick on me. Troy died years ago, but here he was getting on the bus looking exactly the same as the last time I saw him. He looked at me and then he sat down. At first I thought I was having an episode but he was staring at me watching everything I did. I asked the driver Pritchard if he saw the guy staring at me. He nodded yes, I asked him to describe him. "Brown skinned, neat fade, piercing eyes, average tall, average to almost stocky build." When all my passengers were boarded I did my normal tour routine while Pritchard drove. When we got to the Grand Canyon all the passengers except the guy and another guy got off the bus. Pritchard told me to hurry and close the doors before all the air conditioning let out. As soon as I closed the doors Pritchard stood up. He faced the guy, "Larry Bress reporting in." I looked at Pritchard like he was crazy.

"Pamela Latour, my name is Jeremy."

"Jeremy?"

"Yes ma'am. We need to relocate you."

"Me? Why? What's going on?"

Fuzzy's truck pulled up next to the bus. When he got on the bus he froze looking at the guy as well. "Troy?"

"No, I'm not Troy. You were at his funeral." He watched Fuzzy.

"Right, Malcolm called me and told me to get here as soon as possible. What's going on?"

"It's blackout time, does she go with you? Speak now or forever hold your peace."

"She's changed of course she goes with me."

Jeremy took out his phone; "he's taking her with him."

Then he turned the phone towards us and my son's face was on the screen. He was a grown and mature man. Malcolm looked at me with caution. "Fuzzy, you proved me wrong for once. It's blackout time, Jeremy will give you direction."

My heart cried out, "MALCOLM!"

"Yes!"

"I'm sorry for everything!"

"Ok!"

"Thank you!"

"For?"

"Sparing my life."

MORE FROM THE AUTHOR

Thank you for allowing me to entertain you. I hope you have enjoyed reading the third release Beyond The Wallace Series. If you have not read Volumes I – VIII in the Wallace Family Affairs Series, please do so. Checkout my Author Page and stay tuned for more to come shortly.

Volume I Tracy's Complications (Click here)

Volume II Part 1 Sometimes Love Isn't Enough (Click here)

Volume II Part 2 Love Is Just Enough (Click here)

Volume III Invisible (Click here)

Volume IV Look Beyond Your Eyes (Click here)

Volume V No Regrets (Click here)

Volume VI First You Laugh Then You Cry (Click here)

Beyond The Wallace's ~ A Heart That's Taken (Click here)

Volume VII At Last (Click here)

Volume VIII Just A Friend (Click here)

Beyond The Wallace's ~ Abandoned (Click here)
Beyond The Wallace's ~ Distorted Mirrors (Click here)

Beyond The Wallace's ~ Last Words

Once you've enjoyed all of the background stories for our lovely Wallace's and Latour's. Please tune in to the **"Together We Are Strong"** Wallace & Latour Family Seasons and Episodes (Release TBD) on Amazon.